U0144248

洪範譯叢⑩

濟慈詩選

Selected Poems of John Keats

查良錚　譯

洪範書店

臺灣　臺北

濟慈詩選
Selected Poems of John Keats
譯　者　查良錚

發行人　孫致兒

洪範書店有限公司

台北市廈門街113巷17-1號二樓

電話　（02）2365-7577・2368-6790

傳眞　（02）2368-3001

郵撥　01074020

E mail：hung-fan @yahoo.com.tw

行政院新聞局局版臺業字第1425號

初　版　2002年4月

定價250元　ISBN　957-674-222-6

● 漢譯版權所有翻印必究

國家圖書館出版品預行編目資料

濟慈詩選＝Selected Poems of John Keats/
查良錚譯. --初版. --臺北市：洪範,
2002〔民91〕
面；　公分. --（洪範譯叢：10）
中英對照
ISBN 957-674-222-6(平裝)
873.51　　　　　　　　　　　91003665

目 次

譯者序

　　約翰・濟慈（John Keats, 1795─1821）是英國十九世紀浪漫主義運動的傑出詩人，和拜倫、雪萊並稱於世。他出生在倫敦，父親是一個馬廄主人；詩人的家庭和出身在當時社會看來是相當卑微的，他的一生也無時不在貧困中。在濟慈還不到十五歲的時候，父親已先後去世，他和兩弟一妹在親族和監護人的看管下成長起來。

　　濟慈很早便喜好文學，但是沒有機會求學深造；在他不及十六歲時，便離開學校，給艾得芒頓的一個醫生作學徒。以後他又在倫敦一家醫院中學習兩年，1816年獲得了助理醫師的資格。但濟慈熱愛文學，終於放棄行醫而選擇了寫作和貧困的生活道路。

　　早在學校時期，他就從友人查理士・考登・克拉克那裏借閱了很多文學書籍。最使他傾心的，是英國十七世紀詩人斯賓塞的《仙后》和賈浦曼譯的荷馬史詩。莎士比亞和伊利莎白時代的詩人也是被他讀了又讀的。他仿照斯賓塞的風格寫出早期的一些作品。由於和當時的自由主義者和民主主義者的往還，他結識了作家李・漢特，又通過他認識了雪萊及其他作家。漢特很看重濟慈的詩才，在他所主編的自由主義刊物《探索者》上面，在1816年5月，首次發表了濟慈的詩作 ── 十四行詩〈啊，孤獨〉。1817年，由於雪萊的幫助，他出版了第一本詩集，其中包括他自1813年以來四年中所寫的詩。但這本詩集的出版在文壇上受到異常的冷落。

　　1818年，他的長詩〈安狄米恩〉問世。由於他和漢特的親密關係，由於他平日進步的政治見解，還更由於這首長詩的自由思想和反古典主義傾向，他受到了保守雜誌和評論家的攻擊。

最初，濟慈和漢特有共同的政治傾向和文學嗜好，他們都喜愛斯賓塞、文藝復興時期的詩和古代神話。在〈睡與詩〉中，濟慈所宣告的反古典主義的詩的信條也反映了漢特的批評見解。但濟慈早年詩歌創作上的弱點，卻正是受了漢特詩作的不良影響而發展起來的，自1818年以後才逐漸克服。在政治見解方面，他和漢特的接近也沒有多久，很快就對原有的政見幻滅了。

1818—19年是詩人生活最痛苦、同時創作力也是最旺盛和趨於成熟的時期。一方面，保守雜誌在對他口誅筆伐；另一方面，他的弟弟托姆的肺病已成了不治之症，他自己得帶著肺病來服侍他，終至看他在1818年12月死去了。這以後不過數星期，他熱戀上一個少女，范妮·勃朗。這是無望的愛情，因為他既沒有經濟能力和她結婚，而且他的健康，他也已預見到，是不會使他活多久的。就在這種情況下，他努力於寫作，除試寫戲劇（《奧托大帝》）外，還寫有長詩〈伊莎貝拉〉、〈海披里安〉、〈聖亞尼節的前夕〉和〈拉米亞〉等。他最著稱的頌詩如〈希臘古甕頌〉、〈夜鶯頌〉、〈秋頌〉，民歌體詩如〈無情的妖女〉以及很多優美的十四行詩都是在這期間寫成的。

1820年，濟慈的肺病趨於惡化，使他不得不停筆。9月，他接受友人的勸告去到義大利養病。但到義大利不久，即在1821年2月去世了，死時才二十五歲。在他的墓碑上，友人按照他的遺言銘刻了如下一句話：「這裏安息了一個把名字寫在水上的人。」雪萊曾寫有〈阿童尼〉一首長詩哀悼詩人的死亡。

總起來看，濟慈的創作生涯不過短短五年，而且是青年時代的五年，雖然這五年已經給英國和世界文學的寶庫留下了珍貴的遺產。可惜的是，詩人終竟宏才未展而就夭折了。他自題的墓銘已經

表示他感覺到了這一點。他的早死，自然是和他所生活於其中的社會制度、和保守派對他的直接和間接的打擊分不開的。拜倫早已有見於此，他在《唐璜》的第十一章中寫道：

> 濟慈被一篇批評殺死了，
> 正當他可望寫出偉大的作品；
> 儘管晦澀，他曾經力圖談到
> 希臘的神祇，使他們在如今
> 呈現他們該呈現的面貌。
> 可憐的人，多乖戾的命運！
> 他那心靈，那火焰的顆粒，
> 竟讓一篇文章把自己吹熄。

　　拜倫和雪萊對濟慈的同情和愛惜，絕不是偶然的。我們知道，在十九世紀後半葉的英國，濟慈的詩的影響凌駕一切十九世紀詩人之上，形成了當時詩歌的主要的流派。

　　在早期作品中，有明顯地表現社會題材的詩如〈詠和平〉、〈寫於李‧漢特先生出監之日〉、〈給海登〉、〈憤於世人的迷信而作〉、〈致克蘇斯珂〉等。這些詩流露了詩人的社會意識以及對現實的不滿。

　　但是另一方面，他也企圖以自然、藝術和感官的享受構成一幅快樂的生活圖畫，而將這想像的感官世界置於現實世界之上。他彷彿說，現實世界是悲慘的、醜陋的，這是它不值得注視的一面；可是還有美和美感在，讓我們去追求這種快樂吧，因為這是更高的眞實。因此，在〈希臘古甕頌〉裏，他寫下「美即是眞，眞即是美」

這句話來。

　　濟慈不是革命的浪漫主義者，沒有在詩中提出改造現實生活的課題，作品也不像拜倫及雪萊那樣尖刻而多方面反映現實；但另一方面，他也和湖畔詩人們不同，即使只就「描寫美」這一點而言；因爲他所追求的美和美感，不在於神秘主義的、縹緲的境界（如柯勒律治），不在過去或另一個世界裏，而就在現實現象中。他從熱愛現在、熱愛生活出發，他所歌頌的美感是具體的、眞實的，因此有其相當健康的一面。他善於從瞬息萬變的現實世界掌握並突現其優美的一面，而他認爲，正因爲這「優美」的好景不常，它就更爲優美，更值得人以感官去盡情宴饗 —— 濟慈的詩在探索這樣一種生活感受上達到了藝術的高峰。

　　濟慈對自然及生命，在早期一篇傑出的詩作〈蟈蟈和蟋蟀〉裏很清楚地表現出來。在這首小詩裏，他眞實地傳達出夏日郊野和冬季室內的兩種景色，寫出了他對生命運行不息和自然間永恆的美的感受，通篇充滿了明朗的樂觀情調。〈秋頌〉是這種感覺和情調的繼續發展和成熟。

　　藝術的欣賞是濟慈所常常歌頌的另一種生活感受。我們說它是生活感受，因爲濟慈的心靈對藝術如此飢渴，它對他的生命已經是如陽光和空氣一樣地必需。如果說，早期的〈初讀賈浦曼譯荷馬有感〉還只是表現了對藝術的單純的陶醉，和現實生活聯繫不多；那麼，在後期的〈希臘古甕頌〉中，這種感受已不單純是藝術陶醉，而且滲透著現實感。同樣，在〈夜鶯頌〉中，詩人一面歌頌夜鶯所生活著的世界，一面不斷想到人間；這使他旣喜悅於「永恆的美」，又感到現實的痛苦的重壓；這兩種情緒的衝突貫穿了全詩。

　　他的叙事詩傑作〈聖亞尼節的前夕〉是另一個例子。在這裏，

像羅密歐和朱麗葉一樣年輕而美麗的愛情故事，在充滿敵視的背景中進行。詩人使我們看到，一方面，年輕的戀人如何熱烈地追求光明與溫暖，另一方面，又不時地指出那個粗暴、冷酷、酗酒的世界的存在，它隨時都可以把這美麗的愛情像肥皂泡一樣地戳破。「美」和「現實」是太挨近了，使人不得不感到顫慄和恐懼。這篇詩對於色彩的描寫，對於冷的氣候、月光、臥房陳設和戀人所經歷的各種美妙情景的描寫都達到出神入化的地步，引起了各時代的讀者的讚嘆。還有，成為本詩另一特點的是，它的結尾既不是悲劇，也不是快樂的收場。詩人告訴我們，在遠古，有一對年輕的戀人終於逃進了嚴冬的風雪之中，如此而已。這故事本身就像是對「美」的一支讚歌，悠悠然盤旋在半空，令人神往不已。

無論濟慈的哪一篇詩，都是充滿了熱愛生活的樂觀情調的，這種健康的調子使我們不由得想到普希金的詩。例如，在〈羅賓漢〉這首詩中，詩人一直在惋惜「快樂而古老的英國」的消逝，我們會以為它將以哀歌告終的吧？── 然而不，它最後一轉，樂觀地唱道：

> 儘管他們的日子不再，
> 讓我們唱支歌兒開懷。

明朗，堅韌，而又極其真誠，── 這是多麼可喜的藝術天性！〈憂鬱頌〉也是同樣地把「憂鬱」化成了振奮心靈的歌唱。詩人指出，生活即使是憂鬱的，在憂鬱中也可以見到美，因此也有喜悅。這裏既揭示出他作為詩人的弱點，說明他何以避免和現實作鬥爭，同時也顯示了他是多麼熱愛生活，在逆境中還能保持著樂觀勇毅的

精神。

今天，濟慈在讀者中的聲譽是很高的。我想，這也並非偶然。因爲濟慈所展示給我們的儘管是一個小天地，其中卻沒有拜倫的悲觀和絕望，也沒有雪萊的烏托邦氣氛 —— 它是一個半幻想、半堅實、而又充滿人間溫暖與生活美感的世界。

我所根據的原文，是E. D. 西林考特編訂的《約翰·濟慈詩集》（E. De Sélincourt: *The Poems of John Keats*, 倫敦1905年版）。濟慈的詩在形式上、在語言上都可以說是英文詩中的高峰，譯時力圖在形式上追隨原作，十四行詩和頌詩等都照原來的格式押韻（只有幾處例外），在十四行上面，我更力求每行字數近似，使其看來整齊、精煉。

Dedication

To Leigh Hunt, Esq

G LORY and loveliness have passed away
　　For if we wander out in early morn,
　　No wreathed incense do we see upborne
Into the east, to meet the smiing day :
No crowd of nymphs soft voic'd and young, and gay,
　　In woven baskets bringing ears of corn,
　　Roses, and pinks, and violets, to adorn
The shrine of Flora in her early May.
But there are left delights as high as these,
　　And I shall ever bless my destiny,
That in a time, when under pleasant trees
　　Pan is no longer sought, I feel a free
A leafy luxury, seeing I could please
　　With these poor offerings, a man like thee.

獻　詩*

—— 給李·漢特先生

神奇和瑰麗都已消失、不見；

　　因為啊，當我們在清晨遊蕩，

　　我們不再看見一縷爐香

裊入東方，迎接微笑的白天；

不再有快樂的一群少女

　　妙曼地歌唱，手提著花籃，

　　把穀穗、玫瑰、石竹、紫羅蘭，

攜去裝飾五月的花神祭。

不過，倒還有詩歌這種樂趣

　　遺留下來，點綴平凡的歲月；

我欣幸：在這時代，在林蔭裏

　　固然沒有了牧神，我尚能感覺

蔥蘢的恬美，因為我還能以

　　這束貧乏的獻禮，給你喜悅。

1817年3月

---

* 這首獻詩是印在濟慈第一本詩集的首頁上面的。
　李·漢特（Leigh Hunt, 1784—1859），英國作家及詩人，《探索者》雜誌的主編，他初次
　發表了濟慈的詩，並予以評論。濟慈通過他而認識雪萊。他也是拜倫的友人。

To my Brother George

MANY the wonders I this day have seen :
    The sun, when first he kist away the tears
      That fill'd the eyes of morn ; — the laurel'd peers
Who from the feathery gold of evening lean ; —
The ocean with its vastness, its blue green,
      Its ships, its rocks, its caves, its hopes, its fears, —
      Its voice mysterious, which whoso hears
Must think on what will be, and what has been.
E'en now, dear George, while this for you I write,
      Cynthia is from her silken curtains peeping
So scantly, that it seems her bridal night,
      And she her half-discover'd revels keeping.
But what, without the social thought of thee,
Would be the wonders of the sky and sea ?

給我的弟弟喬治

今天我看見的奇跡很多：
　　初升的旭日吻乾了清晨
　　眼中的淚，天宇中的詩人
憑倚著黃昏輕柔的金色；
我看見碧藍而廣闊的海，
　　它那巉岩，洞穴，海船，憧憬
　　和憂懼，還有神秘的海聲
令人悠悠想到過去和未來！
親愛的喬治啊，就在此時，
　　月神像在她新婚的夜晚，
羞怯地從絲帷向外窺伺，
　　她的歡情還只流露一半。
唉，但天空和海洋的奇跡
算了什麼，若不是聯想到你？

1816年8—9月

To******

HAD I a man's fair form, then might my sighs
    Be echoed swiftly through that ivory shell
    Thine ear, and find thy gentle heart ; so well
Would passion arm me for the enterprize :
But ah! I am no knight whose foeman dies ;
    No cuirass glistens on my bosom's swell ;
    I am no happy shepherd of the dell
Whose lips have trembled with a maiden's eyes.
Yet must I dote upon thee, — call thee sweet,
    Sweeter by far than Hybla's honied roses
        When steep'd in dew rich to intoxication.
Ah ! I will taste that dew, for me 'tis meet,
    And when the moon her pallid face discloses,
        I'll gather some by spells, and incantation.

給——

假如我面貌英俊，我的輕嘆
　　就會迅速蕩過那玲瓏玉殼——
　　你的耳朵，把你的心找到；
熱情儘夠鼓舞我前去冒險：
但可惜我不是無敵的騎士，
　　沒有盔甲閃閃的在我前胸，
　　我也不是山中快樂的牧童，
能讓嘴唇對牧女的眼睛放肆。
然而我仍得愛你，說你甜蜜，
　　因爲你甜過希布拉*的玫瑰
　　當它浸潤在醉人的露水裏。
唉！但我只合品嘗那露滴，
　　等月亮露出臉，蒼白而憔悴，
　　我將要憑咒語把露水採集。

1816年

---

*　希布拉（Hybla），愛特納山腰上的城鎮，有野生芳草，味極甘美。

Written on the day that Mr. Leigh Hunt left Prison

WHAT though, for showing truth to flatter'd state,
    Kind Hunt was shut in prison, yet has he,
      In his immortal spirit, been as free
As the sky-searching lark, and as elate.
Minion of grandeur ! think you he did wait ?
      Think you he nought but prison walls did see,
      Till, so unwilling, thou unturn'dst the key ?
Ah, no ! far happier, nobler was his fate!
In Spenser's halls he strayed, and bowers fair,
      Culling enchanted flowers ; and he flew
With daring Milton through the fields of air :
      To regions of his own his genius true
Took happy flights.   Who shall his fame impair
      When thou art dead, and all thy wretched crew ?

寫於李・漢特先生出監之日 *

為了對當政直言，而不阿諛，
　　和藹的漢特豈能畏懼監禁？
　　因為他和他那不朽的精神
正和雲雀一樣自由而歡欣。
榮華底寵兒啊！是否你以為
　　他只是期待，只是望著牆壁，
　　直到你不情願地打開牢獄？
啊，不！他的命途快樂而高貴！
在斯賓塞 ** 的客廳和亭園中
　　他遊蕩著，採摘魅人的鮮花，
他和密爾頓 *** 在廣闊的高空
　　快樂地飛翔，直抵天才的家。
他的美名能不與世永存？
　　且讓你的一夥逞凶這刹那！

1815年2月

---

* 　李・漢特在《探索者》雜誌上發表評論攝政王的文字，被判處罰金及兩年禁閉。他在
　監獄中繼續編輯工作，友人拜倫等都曾前往獄中探視他。他於1815年2月2日出獄時，
　濟慈曾訪他表示祝賀。
** 　斯賓塞（E. Spenser, 1522?—1599），英國宮廷詩人，著有《仙后》等，以文體綺麗著
　稱。
*** 密爾頓（J. Milton, 1608—1674），清教革命時代的詩人，著有《失樂園》等。

"How many bards gild the lapses of time!"

HOW many bards gild the lapses of time !
⠀⠀A few of them have ever been the food
⠀⠀Of my delighted fancy, — I could brood
Over their beauties, earthly, or sublime :
And often, when I sit me down to rhyme,
⠀⠀These will in throngs before my mind intrude :
⠀⠀But no confusion, no disturbance rude
Do they occasion ; 'tis a pleasing chime.
So the unnumber'd sounds that evening store :
⠀⠀The songs of birds — the whisp'ring of the leaves —
⠀⠀The voice of waters — the great bell that heaves
With solemn sound, — and thousand others more,
⠀⠀That distance of recognizance bereaves,
Make pleasing music, and not wild uproar.

「有多少詩人」

有多少詩人把閒暇鍍成金！
 　我的幻想總愛以詩章作為
 　食品 —— 它平凡或莊嚴的美
能使我默默沉思很多時辰；
平時，每當我坐下來吟詠，
 　詩人就擁聚在我的腦海間，
 　但並不引起蕪雜的騷亂，
而是合唱出悅耳的歌聲。
正如黃昏容納的無數聲音：
 　樹葉的低語，鳥兒的歌唱，
 　水流的潺潺，由暮鐘的振蕩
所發的莊嚴之聲，和千種
 　縹緲得難以辨識的音響，
它們構成絕唱，而不是喧騰。

1816年3月

To a Friend who sent me some Roses

A S late I rambled in the happy fields,
　　What time the sky-lark shakes the tremulous dew
　　From his lush clover covert ; — when anew
Adventurous knights take up their dinted shields :
I saw the sweetest flower wild nature yields,
　　A fresh-blown musk-rose ; 'twas the first that threw
　　Its sweets upon the summer : graceful it grew
As is the wand that queen Titania wields.
And, as I feasted on its fragrancy,
　　I thought the garden-rose it far excell'd :
But when, O Wells ! thy roses came to me
　　My sense with their deliciousness was spell'd :
Soft voices had they, that with tender plea
　　Whisper'd of peace, and truth, and friendliness unquell'd.

給贈我以玫瑰的友人 *

最近，我在愉快的田野裏漫步；
　　天鵝正在茂密的苜蓿蔭翳裏
　　搖落顫動的露珠，冒險的騎士
也正又拿起打凹的盾牌上路；
這時，我看到最美的野生花朵 ——
　　一枝早開的麝香薔薇，在初夏
　　散發著甜香，像女皇泰坦妮亞 **
所執的魔杖，秀麗地滋長著。
當我宴饗於它的芬芳的時候，
　　我想，它遠優於花園裏的玫瑰：
可是，威爾斯啊，你的玫瑰來後，
　　我的感官卻迷於它們的甘美：
它們有輕柔的聲音，悄悄懇求
　　和平、真理、和無盡友情的陶醉。

＊　指查理斯・威爾斯（Charles Wells, 1799—1879），濟慈弟弟托姆的同學，曾寫過一些
　　小說和劇本。
＊＊　泰坦妮亞，妖仙的女皇，見莎士比亞的《仲夏夜之夢》。

To G. A. W.

NYMPH of the downward smile, and sidelong glance,
    In what diviner moments of the day
    Art thou most lovely ? — when gone far astray
Into the labyrinths of sweet utterance,
Or when serenely wand'ring in a trance
    Of sober thought ? — or when starting away
    With careless robe, to meet the morning ray,
Thou spar'st the flowers in thy mazy dance ?
Haply 'tis when thy ruby lips part sweetly,
    And so remain, because thou listenest :
But thou to please wert nurtured so completely
    That I can never tell what mood is best.
I shall as soon pronounce which Grace more neatly
    Trips it before Apollo than the rest.

給G．A．W．*

斜睨和低首微笑的少女啊，
　　在一天中哪個神奇的剎那
　　你最可愛？是否當你在說話，
一片甜蜜的語調令人沉迷？
或者是看你在安靜地思索，
　　默默出神？或者突然起了床，
　　你披著長衫，出去迎接晨光，
一路縱跳，不願意踐踏花朵？
也許最好是看你凝神地
　　張著紅唇聆聽，滿面愛嬌：
但你生得如此討人歡喜，
　　很難說：哪種情致最美妙；
正如難說哪一位格拉茜**
　　在阿波羅***前舞得最輕巧。

1816年12月

＊　　G．A．威里（Georgiana Wylie），以後爲喬治・濟慈（濟慈弟）之妻。
＊＊　格拉茜，大神宙斯的幾個女兒的總稱。她們司美及快樂等。
＊＊＊阿波羅，日神，司藝術。

"O Solitude! if I must with thee dwell"

O SOLITUDE ! if I must with thee dwell,
     Let it not be among the jumbled heap
  Of murky buildings ; climb with me the steep, —
Nature's observatory — whence the dell,
Its flowery slopes, its river's crystal swell,
     May seem a span ; let me thy vigils keep
     'Mongst boughs pavillion'd, where the deer's swift leap
Startles the wild bee from the fox-glove bell.
But though I'll gladly trace these scenes with thee,
     Yet the sweet converse of an innocent mind,
     Whose words are images of thoughts refin'd,
Is my soul's pleasure ; and it sure must be
     Almost the highest bliss of human-kind,
When to thy haunts two kindred spirits flee.

「哦，孤獨」*

哦，孤獨！假若我和你必需
　　同住，可別在這層迭的一片
　　灰色建築裏，讓我們爬上山，
到大自然的觀測台去，從那裏 ──
山谷，晶亮的河，錦簇的草坡，
　　看來只是一搾；讓我守著你
　　在枝葉蔭蔽下，看跳縱的鹿麋
把指頂花盅裏的蜜蜂驚嚇。
不過，雖然我喜歡和你賞玩
　　這些景色，我的心靈更樂於
　　和純潔的心靈（她的言語
是優美情思的表象）親切會談；
　　因爲我相信，人的至高的樂趣
是一對心靈避入你的港灣。

1816年

---

* 這是濟慈第一次發表的詩作，發表在《探索者》上面。

To my Brothers

SMALL, busy flames play through the fresh laid coals,
    And their faint cracklings o' er our silence creep
    Like whispers of the household gods that keep
A gentle empire o' er fraternal souls.
And while, for rhymes, I search around the poles,
    Your eyes are fix'd, as in poetic sleep,
    Upon the lore so voluble and deep,
That aye at fall of night our care condoles.
This is your birth-day Tom, and I rejoice
    That thus it passes smoothly, quietly.
Many such eves of gently whisp' ring noise
    May we together pass, and calmly try
What are this world's true joys, — ere the great voice,
    From its fair face, shall bid our spirits fly.

November 18, 1816.

給我的兄弟們

小小的火苗從新添的煤裏
　　歡跳著，它微弱的爆裂聲音
　　爬過一片靜寂，像冥冥的家神
在對這些友愛的靈魂低語。
當我，為了韻律，向星空覓探，
　　你的眼睛卻帶著詩意的迷醉
　　注視這本大書，它如此深邃，
常在向晚慰解我們的憂煩。
今天是你的生日，托姆，我
　　很高興它過得和煦而靜謐。
但願我們能一起度過很多
　　這樣充滿低語的黃昏，安詳地
品嚐這世界的真正的歡樂，
　　直到上帝的聲音把我們喚去。

　　　　　　　　　1816年11月18日

"Keen, fitful gusts are whisp'ring here and there"

K EEN, fitful gusts are whisp'ring here and there
    Among the bushes half leafless, and dry ;
        The stars look very cold about the sky,
And I have many miles on foot to fare.
Yet feel I little of the cool bleak air,
        Or of the dead leaves rustling drearily,
        Or of those silver lamps that burn on high,
Or of the distance from home's pleasant lair :
For I am brimfull of the friendliness ;
        That in a little cottage I have found ;
Of fair-hair'd Milton's eloquent distress,
        And all his love for gentle Lycid drown'd ;
Of lovely Laura in her light green dress,
        And faithful Petrarch gloriously crown'd.

「陣陣寒風」*

陣陣寒風在叢林裏低吟，
　　樹木的葉子半已剝落，枯凋
　　天空的星斗看來那樣冷峭，
而我還有很多哩路躓行。
可是，我一點都沒感到寒意，
　　也沒想到枯葉的颯颯響聲，
　　或是天空中的盞盞銀燈，
或是返家的遙遠的距離：
因為我洋溢著友情的溫暖，
　　是在一間小村屋裏，我看到 ——
金髮的密爾頓內心的憂煩，
　　為淹死的李西德**情辭滔滔；
可愛的勞拉穿著淺綠長衫，
　　忠實的彼特拉克***冠戴榮耀。

1816年10月

---

* 　這首詩記述濟慈對李‧漢特的一次訪問，他在漢特的「小村屋」裏和漢特談到密爾頓
　　和彼特拉克——他們所喜愛的詩人。
** 　密爾頓的同學及友人愛德華‧金於航海時淹死，密爾頓曾著詩哀悼。李西德即指愛德
　　華‧金。
*** 彼特拉克（Petrarch, 1304—1374），義大利早期文藝復興的詩人，以一組愛情詩著
　　稱，其中所歌頌的少女即勞拉。

"To one who has been long in city pent"

TO one who has been long in city pent,
    'Tis very sweet to look into the fair
    And open face of heaven, — to breathe a prayer
Full in the smile of the blue firmament.
Who is more happy, when, with heart's content,
    Fatigued he sinks into some pleasant lair
    Of wavy grass, and reads a debonair
And gentle tale of love and languishment ?
Returning home at evening, with an ear
    Catching the notes of Philomel, — an eye
Watching the sailing cloudlet's bright career,
    He mourns that day so soon has glided by :
E'en like the passage of an angel's tear
    That falls through the clear ether silently.

「對於一個久居城市的人」

對於一個久居城市的人，
　　看看天空的明媚的面貌，
　　對著蔚藍的蒼穹的微笑
低低發聲禱告，多麼怡情！
他可以滿意地，懶懶躺在
　　一片青草的波浪裏，讀著
　　溫雅而憂鬱的愛情小說，
有什麼能比這個更愉快？
傍晚回家了，一面用耳朵
　　聽夜鶯的歌唱，一面觀看
流雲在空中燦爛地飄過，
　　他會哀悼白天這樣短暫：
它竟像天使的淚珠，滑落
　　清朗的氣層，默默地不見。

1816年6月

On first looking into Chapman's Homer

MUCH have I travell'd in the realms of gold,
    And many goodly states and kingdoms seen ;
  Round many western islands have I been
Which bards in fealty to Apollo hold.
Oft of one wide expanse had I been told
    That deep-brow'd Homer ruled as his demesne ;
    Yet did I never breathe its pure serene
Till I heard Chapman speak out loud and bold :
Then felt I like some watcher of the skies
    When a new planet swims into his ken ;
Or like stout Cortez when with eagle eyes
    He stared at the Pacific — and all his men
Look'd at each other with a wild surmise —
    Silent, upon a peak in Darien.

初讀賈浦曼譯荷馬有感*

我遊歷了很多金色的國度，
　　看過不少好的城邦和王國，
　　還有多少西方的海島，歌者
都已使它們向阿波羅臣服。
我常聽到有一境域，廣闊無垠，
　　智慧的荷馬在那裏稱王，
　　我從未領略它的純淨、安詳，
直到我聽見賈浦曼的聲音
無畏而高昂。於是，我的情感
　　有如觀象家發現了新的星座，
　　或者像考蒂茲，**以鷹隼的眼
凝視著太平洋，而他的同夥
在驚訝的揣測中彼此觀看，
　　盡站在達利安***高峰上，沉默。

1816年10月

---

* 濟慈不懂希臘文，這裏表示他閱讀賈浦曼（G. Chapman. 1559—1634?）英譯的荷馬
　史詩時所感到的喜悅。據蒲伯說，賈浦曼的譯文充滿了「大膽而火熱的精神」。
** 考蒂茲（H. Cortez, 1485—1547），探險家及墨西哥的征服者。實則他不是第一個發
　現太平洋的歐洲人。
*** 達利安（Darien），中美洲的海峽。

On leaving some Friends at an early Hour

GIVE me a golden pen, and let me lean
    On heap'd up flowers, in regions clear, and far ;
  Bring me a tablet whiter than a star,
Or hand of hymning angel, when 'tis seen
The silver strings of heavenly harp atween :
    And let there glide by many a pearly car,
    Pink robes, and wavy hair, and diamond jar,
And half discovered wings, and glances keen.
The while let music wander round my ears,
    And as it reaches each delicious ending,
      Let me write down a line of glorious tone,
And full of many wonders of the spheres :
    For what a height my spirit is contending !
      'Tis not content so soon to be alone.

清晨別友人有感

給我一枝金筆吧，讓我靠守
　　一柱花，在明媚縹緲的境域；
　　給我一塊比星星更晶白的
方石，不然就給我天使的手
好把歌頌天庭的銀弦彈奏：
　　讓珍珠的車駕，粉紅的衣裙，
　　鬆髮，明眸的眼，鑽石的花瓶，
和半顯的翅翼在眼前飄走。
讓樂聲在我的耳邊繚繞，
　　而當每一曲悠悠地告終，
　　讓我寫下哪怕一行輝煌的
音節，充滿天庭的百般美妙：
　　啊，我的心正攀登多高的高峰！
　　它不願這樣快就獨行踽踽。

1816年11月

Addressed to Haydon

HIGHMINDEDNESS, a jealousy for good,
    A loving-kindness for the great man's fame,
    Dwells here and there with people of no name,
In noisome alley, and in pathless wood :
And where we think the truth least understood,
    Oft may be found a "singleness of aim,"
    That ought to frighten into hooded shame
A money-mong'ring, pitiable brood.
How glorious this affection for the cause
    Of stedfast genius, toiling gallantly !
What when a stout unbending champion awes
    Envy, and Malice to their native sty ?
Unnumber'd souls breathe out a still applause,
    Proud to behold him in his country's eye.

給海登*

高尚的情思，對偉大的聲名
　　和對善的愛好，往往出現
　　在沒沒無聞的人們中間，
在喧囂的小巷，荒蕪的叢林；
我們認爲最無知識的人
　　卻常常具有「意志的堅貞」，
　　這該使放債的、盲昧的一群
感到驚詫、羞愧、無地自容。
無畏的天才啊，孜孜不息，
　　你博得了多麼光輝的敬愛！
當一個堅強的志士把惡意
　　和嫉妒，都嚇得顯現了醜態，
相信吧，無數顆心正驕傲於
　　祖國有了他，在無言地喝采。

1816年11月

---

* 海登（B. R. Haydon, 1786—1846），英國畫家，主要繪宗敎及愛國題材的歷史畫，認爲
這對國民有巨大的敎育意義。但他的畫不能售出，終於因忍受不了生活的壓迫而自殺。

Addressed to the same

GREAT spirits now on earth are sojourning ;
    He of the cloud, the cataract, the lake,
  Who on Helvellyn's summit, wide awake,
Catches his freshness from Archangel's wing :
He of the rose, the violet, the spring,
    The social smile, the chain for Freedom's sake :
    And lo ! — whose stedfastness would never take
A meaner sound than Raphael's whispering.
And other spirits there are standing apart
    Upon the forehead of the age to come ;
These, these will give the world another heart,
    And other pulses.   Hear ye not the hum
Of mighty workings ? ——
    Listen awhile ye nations, and be dumb.

給海登*

偉大的靈魂正寄居凡塵；
　那屬於雲、瀑布、和湖水的人，
　他正守在海爾維林**的高峰
要從天使的翅膀獲得清新；
那守著春天、玫瑰和紫羅蘭，
　對人微笑，爲自由受禁的人，
　啊！　他是這樣堅定，他決不肯
採用稍遜於拉菲爾***的語言。
還有另一些靈魂，遠遠站著，
　孤獨地，在未來時代的尖端；
他們將給世界另一種脈搏，
　另一顆心。　你們難道沒聽見
那巨大進程的前奏？──
　聽一聽吧，世界該啞口無言。

1816年11月

---

　*　本詩前八行所指的人爲華滋華斯，漢特及海登。
　**　海爾維林（Helvellyn），英國北部的山峰。
***　拉菲爾（Raphael, 1483─1520），義大利文藝復興時期的偉大畫家。

On the Grasshopper and Cricket

THE poetry of earth is never dead :
  When all the birds are faint with the hot sun,
    And hide in cooling trees, a voice will run
From hedge to hedge about the new-mown mead ;
That is the Grasshopper's — he takes the lead
  In summer luxury, — he has never done
    With his delights ; for when tired out with fun
He rests at ease beneath some pleasant weed.
The poetry of earth is ceasing never :
  On a lone winter evening, when the frost
    Has wrought a silence, from the stove there shrills
The Cricket's song, in warmth increasing ever,
  And seems to one in drowsiness half lost,
    The Grasshopper's among some grassy hills.

December 30, 1816.

蟈蟈和蟋蟀

從不間斷的是大地的詩歌：
　　當鳥兒疲於炎熱的太陽
　　在樹蔭裏沉默，在草地上
就另有種聲音從籬笆飄過；
那是蟈蟈的歌聲，它急於
　　享受夏日的盛宴的喜悅，
　　唱個不停；而等它需要停歇，
就在青草叢裏稍稍憩息。
啊，大地的詩歌從不間斷：
　　在孤寂的冬夜，當冰霜凍結，
　　　　四周靜悄悄，爐邊就響起了
蟋蟀的歌聲，而室中的溫暖
　　使人矇矓欲睡，我們會感覺
　　　　彷彿是蟈蟈在山坡上鳴叫。

1816年12月30日

To Kosciusko

GOOD Kosciusko, thy great name alone
 Is a full harvest whence to reap high feeling ;
 It comes upon us like the glorious pealing
Of the wide spheres — an everlasting tone.
And now it tells me, that in worlds unknown,
 The names of heroes burst from clouds concealing,
 And change to harmonies, for ever stealing
Through cloudless blue, and round each silver throne.
It tells me too, that on a happy day,
 When some good spirit walks upon the earth,
 Thy name with Alfred's, and the great of yore
 Gently commingling, gives tremendous birth
To a loud hymn, that sounds far, far away
 To where the great God lives for evermore.

34

致克蘇斯珂*

克蘇斯珂啊！你偉大的名字
　是一次豐收集起高貴的感情；
　對於我們，它是輝煌的樂音
來自天宇：一支永恆的調子。
它告訴了我，在未知的世界中，
　有些英雄的名字自陰雲間
　爆發出來，變爲樂聲，就永遠
盤旋在星際和無垠的天空。
它又告訴我，在歡樂的日子，
　當世上行走著善良的精靈，
　　你的、阿弗瑞德**的、和古昔
　偉人的名字，就會合而產生
一曲響亮的、柔和的讚美詩，
　　它將遠遠飄蕩，直達於上帝。

1816年12月

* 克蘇斯珂（Kosciusko, ?—1817），波蘭的愛國志士，曾參加美國獨立戰爭，並爲了爭
　取波蘭的自由，在1792年率領四千人抵抗俄軍一萬六千人。波蘭屈服後，他於1794年
　再起而抵抗俄普聯軍，失敗被俘。被釋後卜居倫敦及巴黎，享受著自由戰士的榮耀。
** 阿弗瑞德（Alfred, 849—901），撒克遜王，以開明著稱。他曾振興文學，並譯有哲學
　及歷史著作多種。

35

"Happy is England"

HAPPY is England!   I could be content
    To see no other verdure than its own ;
   To feel no other breezes than are blown
Through its tall woods with high romances blent :
Yet do I sometimes feel a languishment
    For skies Italian, and an inward groan
    To sit upon an Alp as on a throne,
And half forget what world or worldling meant.
Happy is England, sweet her artless daughters ;
    Enough their simple loveliness for me,
      Enough their whitest arms in silence clinging :
    Yet do I often warmly burn to see
      Beauties of deeper glance, and hear their singing,
And float with them about the summer waters.

「快樂的英國」

快樂的英國！　我足夠滿意了，
　　不必再看別處的綠草如茵，
　　在它傳說中的高大的樹林，
吹拂的風足夠伴著我逍遙。
不過，我還有時鬱鬱地懷戀
　　義大利的天空，我內心渴望
　　把阿爾卑斯山當王位坐上，
使我好似忘了世界和人寰。
快樂的英國，它無邪的姑娘
　　純眞、嫵媚，應該足使我心歡
　　　默默挽著她們那潔白的臂膀：
　　可是啊，我還時常想要去觀看
　　　黑眼睛的美女，聽她們歌唱，
並且一起在夏日的湖中游蕩。

To Chatterton

O CHATTERTON ! how very sad thy fate !
　　Dear child of sorrow — son of misery !
　How soon the film of death obscur'd that eye,
Whence Genius mildly flash'd, and high debate.
How soon that voice, majestic and elate,
　　Melted in dying numbers !　Oh ! how nigh
　　Was night to thy fair morning.　Thou didst die
A half-blown flow'ret which cold blasts amate.
But this is past : thou art among the stars
　　Of highest Heaven : to the rolling spheres
Thou sweetly singest : nought thy hymning mars,
　　Above the ingrate world and human fears.
On earth the good man base detraction bars
　　From thy fair name, and waters it with tears.

致查特頓*

查特頓！憂傷和苦難之子！
　啊，你的命運是多麼悲慘！
　天才和崇高的爭論徒然
在你眼裏閃爍，過早的死
已使它幽暗！那莊嚴的歌
　　這麼快逝去了！　夜這樣逼近
　　你美麗的早晨。　一陣寒風
使尚未盛開的小花凋落。
但這已成為過去：而今，你
　　住在星空，對著旋轉的蒼穹
美妙地歌唱，不再受制於
　　人心的憂懼和忘恩的人群。
在地面，好人正捍衛你的名字，
　　並且要以淚水把它滋潤。

1814年

---

* 查特頓（T. Chatterton, 1752—1770），英國文學史上壽命最短的詩人。他捏造了很多英
國古代的文件及著作，偽托若雷之名寫了很多詩發表出來，並且寫有歌劇上演。但終於
因貧困不得意而服毒自殺，死時年僅十七歲。他的詩雖偽托古人之作，但頗見他自己的
詩才，以後合訂成集，出版多次。

To Byron

BYRON ! how sweetly sad thy melody !
     Attuning still the soul to tenderness,
     As if soft Pity, with unusual stress,
Had touch'd her plaintive lute, and thou, being by,
Hadst caught the tones, nor suffer'd them to die.
     O'ershadowing sorrow doth not make thee less
     Delightful : thou thy griefs dost dress
With a bright halo, shining beamily,
As when a cloud the golden moon doth veil,
     Its sides are ting'd with a resplendent glow,
Through the dark robe oft amber rays prevail,
     And like fair veins in sable marble flow ;
Still warble, dying swan ! still tell the tale,
     The enchanting tale, the tale of pleasing woe.

給拜倫

拜倫！你的歌聲多麼甜蜜
　　而悒鬱，教人心裏生出溫情，
　　彷彿是「悲憫」曾彈低訴的琴，
你聽到了，便把那音階銘記，
使它得以流傳。幽暗的悲傷
　　並沒有使你的魅力減少；
　　在你的悲哀上，你給覆蓋了
一輪光暈，使它燦然放光，
彷彿是遮住滿月的雲霧，
　　它的邊緣鑲著耀眼的黃金，
琥珀的光輝從黑袍下透出，
　　又似烏雲石上美麗的脈紋；
垂死的天鵝啊，請娓娓地唱，
　　唱你的故事，你悅人的悲傷。

1814年

41

On Peace

O PEACE ! and dost thou with thy presence bless
   The dwellings of this war-surrounded Isle ;
Soothing with placid brow our late distress,
Making the triple kingdom brightly smile ?
Joyful I hail thy presence ; and I hail
The sweet companions that await on thee ;
Complete my joy — let not my first wish fail,
Let the sweet mountain nymph thy favourite be,
With England's happiness proclaim Europa's Liberty.
O Europe ! let not sceptred tyrants see
That thou must shelter in thy former state ;
Keep thy chains burst, and boldly say thou art free ;
Give thy kings law — leave not uncurbed the (great ?)
So with the honours past thou'lt win thy happier fate !

詠和平*

和平啊！你可是來祝福
這被戰爭環繞的海島，
以你靜謐的面容來平復
我們的憂慮，使三邦微笑？
我快樂地迎接你，我歡呼
隨你蒞臨的優美的伴侶，
請不要把我的初願辜負；
請鍾愛那甜蜜的山林仙女，**
讓英國快樂，歐洲得以自由。
啊，歐羅巴，別使暴君以為
你還得在昔日情況下偷生；
說你要自由，把枷鎖打碎，
給國王法律，別任他們不馴：
那你才能有更美好的命運！

1814年

* 這首詩是在拿破崙戰爭剛剛結束時寫成的。
** 指自由女神。

"Woman! when I behold thee flippant, vain"

WOMAN ! when I behold thee flippant, vain,
    Inconstant, childish, proud, and full of fancies ;
  Without that modest softening that enhances
The downcast eye, repentant of the pain
That its mild light creates to heal again :
    E'en then, elate, my spirit leaps, and prances,
    E'en then my soul with exultation dances
For that to love, so long, I've dormant lain :
But when I see thee meek, and kind, and tender,
    Heavens ! how desperately do I adore
Thy winning graces ; — to be thy defender
    I hotly burn — to be a Calidore —
A very Red Cross Knight — a stout Leander —
    Might I be loved by thee like these of yore.

「女人！當我看到你」

女人！當我看到你虛榮、饒舌、
　　無常、幼稚、驕傲、充滿了夢幻；
　　沒有一絲脈脈的柔情裝點
你那垂目而閃的動人的光澤，
它既然引起，就該醫治心痛：
　　啊，儘管如此，我的心還是歡跳，
　　我的靈魂也在快樂地舞蹈，
因為我久已冬眠，等待愛情；
可是，當我看到你多情、溫和，
　　天哪！我會怎樣全心去崇拜
你迷人的優美；我渴望充作
　　一個紅十字的騎士，衛護在
你的身側，像凱利多，利安德，*
　　我真願和他們似地為你所愛。

1815年

---

* 凱利多是斯賓塞《仙后》中的除妖的騎士。利安德為了去會見他所愛的希羅，每夜游泳
　渡過希臘海峽，終有一夜因遇風暴而淹死。

Written in Disgust of Vulgar Superstition

THE church bells toll a melancholy round,
    Calling the people to some other prayers,
    Some other gloominess, more dreadful cares,
More hearkening to the sermon's horrid sound.
Surely the mind of man is closely bound
    In some black spell ; seeing that each one tears
    Himself from fireside joys, and Lydian airs,
And converse high of those with glory crown'd.
Still, still they toll, and I should feel a damp, —
    A chill as from a tomb, did I not know
That they are dying like an outburnt lamp ;
    That 'tis their sighing, wailing ere they go
    Into oblivion ; — that fresh flowers will grow,
And many glories of immortal stamp.

憤於世人的迷信而作

教堂的鐘聲在陰沉地振盪，
　　它號召人去尋找另一種幽暗，
　　另一種希望，更愁慘的憂煩，
以便傾聽那可惡的宣講。
人的頭腦一定被某種魔咒
　　緊緊縛住了；你不見每個人
　　都匆忙地離開爐邊的歡欣，
拋下柔情的歌，心靈的感受？
那鐘聲盡在響，使我幾乎
　　墜入墳墓散發的陰冷中，
幸而我知道，他們像殘燭
　　就要完了，這是他們的悲聲
　　在沒落之前，而世界將出生
鮮花，和許多燦爛不朽的事物。

　　　　　　　　　　　　1816年12月

"Oh ! how I love"

OH ! how I love, on a fair summer's eve,
    When streams of light pour down the golden west,
  And on the balmy zephyrs tranquil rest
The silver clouds, far — far away to leave
All meaner thoughts, and take a sweet reprieve
    From little cares ; to find, with easy quest,
    A fragrant wild, with Nature's beauty drest,
And there into delight my soul deceive.
There warm my breast with patriotic lore,
    Musing on Milton's fate — on Sydney's bier —
Till their stern forms before my mind arise :
Perhaps on wing of Poesy upsoar,
    Full often dropping a delicious tear,
When some melodious sorrow spells mine eyes.

「啊，在夏日的黃昏」

啊，在夏日的黃昏，當晚霞
　　向西方傾注著萬道金光，
　　當白雲歇在和煦的西風上，
我多願意遠遠地、遠遠拋下
一切卑微的念頭，暫時擺脫
　　小小的顧慮，好隨處去尋覓
　　芬芳的野景，自然的秀麗，
把我的心靈騙入一刻歡樂。
我願意用過去的愛國事跡
　　溫暖自己的心，冥想錫德尼
冷酷的屍架，密爾頓的命運，*
或許我還能借助詩的羽翼
　　而翱翔，並且流灑溫馨的淚，
若是嘹亮的憂傷迷住了眼睛。

1816年

"After dark vapours"

A FTER dark vapours have oppress'd our plains
    For a long dreary season, comes a day
    Born of the gentle South, and clears away
From the sick heavens all unseemly stains.
The anxious month, relieved of its pains,
    Takes as a long-lost right the feel of May,
    The eye-lids with the passing coolness play,
Like rose-leaves with the drip of summer rains.
And calmest thoughts come round us — as of leaves
    Budding — fruit ripening in stillness — autumn suns
Smiling at eve upon the quiet sheaves, —
Sweet Sappho's cheek, — a sleeping infant's breath, —
    The gradual sand that through an hour-glass runs, —
A woodland rivulet, — a Poet's death.

「漫長的冬季」

漫長的冬季才盡，當濃霧
　　不再低壓著我們的平原，
　　從溫煦的南方就送來晴天，
給病懨的天空除盡了斑污。
這解除了痛苦的日子，急於
　　享受權利，已披上五月的感覺，
　　而眼瞼卻還有寒氣在跳躍，
像是玫瑰葉上滴濺的夏雨。
最恬靜的思緒浮蕩在心上，
　　使人想起嫩葉、靜靜成熟的
果實、屋檐上向晚的秋陽、
莎弗*的面頰、睡嬰的呼吸、
　　沙漏中逐漸滴下的沙子、
森林裏的小河、詩人的死。

1817年1月31日

---

* 莎弗（Sappho），古希臘的女詩人，寫有很多愛情詩。

Written on the blank space of a leaf at the end of Chaucer's tale of The Florvre and the Lefe

THIS pleasant tale is like a little copse :
　　The honied lines so freshly interlace,
　　To keep the reader in so sweet a place,
So that he here and there full-hearted stops ;
And oftentimes he feels the dewy drops
　　Come cool and suddenly against his face,
　　And, by the wandering melody, may trace
Which way the tender-legged linnet hops.
Oh ! what a power has white simplicity !
　　What mighty power has this gentle story !
　　I, that do ever feel athirst for glory,
Could at this moment be content to lie
　　Meekly upon the grass, as those whose sobbings
　　Were heard of none beside the mournful robins.

寫在喬叟《花與葉的故事》的
末頁空白上

這可愛的故事像個小叢林：

 甜蜜的辭句如此翠綠交纏，

 讀者關在小小的天地裏面

感到如此美妙，他常常全心

停下來瀏灠，而清涼的露滴

 有時會不意地落在臉上，

 他也可以循著歌聲的迴蕩

看細腳的紅雀向何處跳去。

啊，晶瑩的單純是多麼動人！

 這文雅的故事多富於魅力！

 而我，儘管總是渴求榮譽，

這一刻，卻滿足地躺在草中，

 就像那兩個孩子，與世隔離，

 只有知更鳥聽他們的哭泣。*

1817年2月

---

* 最後兩句影射英國古代民歌的一個故事。那故事說，一個鄉紳臨死時把一兒一女托付其
弟照管，弟弟圖財，雇了兩個惡徒將兩個孩子騙入樹林，以便殺死。但惡徒終於不忍下
手而遁去。孩子們餓死林中，知更鳥以樹葉把他們掩埋起來。

On seeing the Elgin Marbles for the first time

My spirit is too weak ; mortality
   Weighs heavily on me like unwilling sleep,
    An each imagined pinnacle and steep
Of godlike hardship tells me I must die
Like a sick eagle looking at the sky.
    Yet 'tis a gentle luxury to weep,
    That I have not the cloudy winds to keep
Fresh for the opening of the morning's eye.
Such dim-conceived glories of the brain
    Bring round the heart an indescribable feud ;
So do these wonders a most dizzy pain,
    That mingles Grecian grandeur with the rude
Wasting of old Time — with a billowy main
    A sun, a shadow of a magnitude.

初見愛爾金壁石有感*

我的心靈是脆弱的；無常
　　重壓著我，像不情願的夢，
　　每件神工底玄想的極峰
都在告訴我，我必將死亡，
像仰望天空的一隻病鷹。
　　可是，哭泣又未免太過分，
　　即使不能凌駕雲霄的風
去迎接剛剛睜眼的清晨。
這極盡想像的輝煌之作
　　給我滋生了難言的矛盾：
希臘的光輝終於越過
　　時流的摧殘，眩人心神，
我看見的是灰色的浪波，
　　卻也有太陽，有一痕雄渾。

1817年2月

---

* 希臘神殿的古壁畫及雕飾被英國人愛爾金劫至英國，因稱為「愛爾金壁石」，置於大英博
　物館中。

55

On the Sea

IT keeps eternal whisperings around
     Desolate shores, and with its mighty swell
    Gluts twice ten thousand caverns, till the spell
Of Hecate leaves them their old shadowy sound.
Often 'tis in such gentle temper found,
     That scarcely will the very smallest shell
     Be moved for days from where it sometime fell,
When last the winds of heaven were unbound.
O ye ! who have your eye-balls vex'd and tired,
     Feast them upon the wideness of the Sea ;
O ye ! whose ears are dinn'd with uproar rude,
     Or fed too much with cloying melody, —
Sit ye near some old cavern's mouth, and brood
Until ye start, as if the sea-nymphs quired !

詠海

沿著荒涼的海岸，它發出
　　永恆的喋喋；有時潮水洶湧，
　　它就加倍淹沒了千萬岩洞，
直到又被赫凱蒂*的魔符
所迷，覆歸於喃喃的波聲；
　　在這種時候，你往往看到
　　曾由狂飆捲來的小小貝殼
會靜止多日，動也不動。
啊，請放眼於大海的廣闊，
　　假如你的雙目迷惑、厭倦；
假如你的耳朵苦於喧騰
　　或嫋嫋之音，請坐在洞邊
默默沉思吧，直到你一驚：
彷彿有海中仙女在唱歌！

1817年

---

* 赫凱蒂，希臘神話中主宰魔咒與鬼魅的女神。

On Leigh Hunt's Poem, The Story of Rimini

WHO loves to peer up at the morning sun,
   With half-shut eyes and comfortable cheek,
      Let him, with this sweet tale, full often seek
For meadows where the little rivers run ;
Who loves to linger with that brightest one
      Of Heaven — Hesperus — let him lowly speak
      These numbers to the night, and starlight meek,
Or moon, if that her hunting be begun.
He who knows these delights, and too is prone
      To moralise upon a smile or tear,
Will find at once a region of his own,
      A bower for his spirit, and will steer
To alleys, where the fir-tree drops its cone,
      Where robins hop, and fallen leaves are sear.

題李·漢特的詩《理敏尼的故事》

誰若是愛對著早晨的太陽，
　　半閉起眼睛，樂於享受閒適，
　　他盡可攜帶這甜蜜的故事
去尋覓草坪和溪水的蕩漾；
誰若是愛守望最明亮的星 ──
　　長庚，── 他盡可把這詩的音節
　　悄悄地念給星光和幽夜，
或月亮，若是她已經在巡行。
誰若懂得這些樂趣，並慣於
　　以一笑或一淚去詮釋世情，
他會在這詩裏找到一片園地 ──
　　他心靈的亭蔭，而且會踱進
許多幽徑裏，看樅樹掉果實，
　　落葉萎黃，還有知更鳥在跳縱。

1817年

On sitting down to read King Lear once again

O GOLDEN-TONGUED Romance with serene lute !
   Fair plumed Syren ! Queen of far away !
   Leave melodizing on this wintry day,
Shut up thine olden pages, and be mute :
Adieu ! for once again the fierce dispute,
   Betwixt damnation and impassion'd clay
   Must I burn through ; once more humbly assay
The bitter-sweet of this Shakespearian fruit.
Chief Poet ! and ye clouds of Albion,
   Begetters of our deep eternal theme,
When through the old oak forest I am gone,
   Let me not wander in a barren dream,
But when I am consumed in the fire,
Give me new Phœnix wings to fly at my desire.

再讀《李耳王》之前有感

哦，金嗓子的傳奇，幽靜的琵琶！
　　美麗的鮫人！縹緲之境的仙后！
　　別在冬天鳴囀你誘人的歌喉，
合上你過時的書頁，安靜吧：
再見了！我得再一次掙扎過
　　高昂的人性與永劫之間的
　　火熱的爭執；我得再細心嘗試
莎士比亞這枚苦澀的甘果。
主導的詩人！阿爾比安*的雲霄！
　　你創始了深刻而永恆的主題；
我就要進入你的古橡樹林了，
　　可別讓我夢遊得徒然無益：
當我在火裏焚燒，請給我裝上
鳳凰的羽翼，好順我的願心飛翔。

1818年

---

* 阿爾比安（Albion），英國古稱。

"When I have fears"

WHEN I have fears that I may cease to be
  Before my pen has glean'd my teeming brain,
Before high-piled books, in charact'ry,
    Hold like full garners the full-ripen'd grain ;
When I behold, upon the night's starr'd face,
    Huge cloudy symbols of a high romance,
And think that I may never live to trace
    Their shadows, with the magic hand of chance ;
And when I feel, fair creature of an hour !
    That I shall never look upon thee more,
Never have relish in the faery power
    Of unreflecting love ! — then on the shore
Of the wide world I stand alone, and think,
Till Love and Fame to nothingness do sink.

「每當我害怕」

每當我害怕，生命也許等不及

　　我的筆蒐集完我蓬勃的思潮，

等不及高高一堆書，在文字裏，

　　像豐富的穀倉，把熟穀子收好；

每當我在繁星的夜幕上看見

　　傳奇故事的巨大的雲霧徵象，

而且想，我或許活不到那一天，

　　以偶然底神筆描出它的幻相；

每當我感覺，啊，瞬息的美人！

　　我也許永遠不會再看到你，

不會再陶醉於無憂的愛情

　　和它的魅力！ —— 於是，在這廣大的

世界的岸沿，我獨自站定、沉思，

直到愛情、聲名、都沒入虛無裏。

1818年1月

To the Nile

SON of the old moon-mountains African !
      Stream of the Pyramid and Crocodile !
We call thee fruitful, and, that very while
A desert fills our seeing's inward span.
Nurse of swart nations since the world began,
Art thou so fruitful ? or dost thou beguile
Those men to honour thee, who, worn with toil,
Rest them a space 'twixt Cairo and Decan ?
O may dark fancies err !   They surely do ;
'Tis ignorance that makes a barren waste
Of all beyond itself.   Thou dost bedew
Green rushes like our rivers, and dost taste
The pleasant sun-rise.   Green isles hast thou too,
And to the sea as happily dost haste.

致尼羅河

背負金字塔和鱷魚的大河！
阿非利加的古月山的兒子！
我們都說你富饒，但同時
我們腦中又浮現一片荒漠。
你養育過多少黝黑的民族，
豈能不富饒？或者，你的風景
難道只使開羅以南的農民
在歇息片刻時，才對你仰慕？
啊，但願無憑的猜想錯了！
只有愚昧才意度自己以外
都是荒涼。　你必潤澤一片蘆草，
和我們的河一樣；晨曦的光彩
必也沾到你，　你也有青綠的島，
而且，也一定快樂地奔向大海。

1818年2月4日

To Spenser

SPENSER ! a jealous honourer of thine,
    A forester deep in thy midmost trees,
Did, last eve, ask my promise to refine
    Some English, that might strive thine ear to please.
    But, Elfin-poet ! 'tis impossible
For an inhabitant of wintry earth
    To rise, like Phœbus, with a golden quill,
Fire-wing'd, and make a morning in his mirth.
    It is impossible to 'scape from toil
O' the sudden, and receive thy spiriting :
    The flower must drink the nature of the soil
Before it can put forth its blossoming :
    Be with me in the summer days, and I
    Will for thine honour and his pleasure try.

致斯賓塞

斯賓塞！你的一個崇拜者，

　　一個深居你的園林中的人，

昨晚要我取悅你的耳朵，

　　寫一篇或許爲你喜愛的英文。

　　但是，靈氣的詩人啊，請想：

一個卜居多之大地的人

　　怎能像日神展開火的翅膀，

手執金筆，快樂地逍遙一早晨？

　　他無法擺脫時令的苦役，

你的鼓舞他還承接不下：

　　一朵花必須受土質的培育，

然後才開出燦爛的鮮葩：

　　等夏天找我吧，爲了敬愛你

　　和取悅他，*那時我將試一試筆。

1818年2月5日

---

* 可能指李·漢特。

To ——

TIME'S sea hath been five years at its slow ebb ;
    Long hours have to and fro let creep the sand ;
Since I was tangled in thy beauty's web,
    And snared by the ungloving of thine hand.
And yet I never look on midnight sky,
    But I behold thine eyes' well memoried light ;
I cannot look upon the rose's dye,
    But to thy cheek my soul doth take its flight ;
I cannot look on any budding flower,
    But my fond ear, in fancy at thy lips,
And hearkening for a love-sound, doth devour
    Its sweets in the wrong sense : —— Thou dost eclipse
Every delight with sweet remembering,
And grief unto my darling joys dost bring.

給 —— *

自從我被你的美所糾纏，
　　你裸露了的手臂把我俘獲，
時間的海洋已經有五年
　　在低潮，沙漏反覆過濾著時刻。
可是，每當我凝視著夜空，
　　我仍看到你的眼睛在閃亮；
每當我看到玫瑰的鮮紅，
　　心靈就朝向你的面頰飛翔；
每當我看到初開放的花，
　　我的耳朵，彷彿貼近你唇際
想聽一句愛語，就會吞下
　　錯誤的芬芳：唉，甜蜜的回憶
使每一種喜悅都黯淡無光，
你給我的歡樂帶來了憂傷。

1818年2月

* 這首詩所給的人，據說是濟慈在狐廳花園中曾偶爾一見的一個女子。

"O that a week could be an age"

O THAT a week could be an age, and we
　　Felt parting and warm meeting every week,
Then one poor year a thousand years would be,
　　The flush of welcome ever on the cheek :
So could we live long life in little space,
　　So time itself would be annihilate,
So a day's journey in oblivious haze
　　To serve our joys would lengthen and dilate.
O to arrive each Monday morn from Ind !
　　To land each Tuesday from the rich Levant !
In little time a host of joys to bind,
　　And keep our souls in one eternal pant !
This morn, my friend, and yester-evening taught
Me how to harbour such a happy thought.

「但願一星期能變成一世紀」

但願一星期能變成一世紀，
　　每周都有感於離別和會見，
那麼，頰上會永遠閃著情誼，
　　短短的一歲就變成一千年；
要是這樣，儘管人生短暫，
　　我們必能長生，時間會無用，
一天的行程會延長和變緩，
　　在朦朧中常保我們的歡情。
但願每星期一都來自印度，
　　星期二返自地中海的旅程，
那麼一瞬間，就有歡樂無數
　　使我們的心靈永恆地激動！
今早和昨晚，朋友，教給了
我該如何珍惜這愉快的思潮。

1818年2－3月

71

The Human Seasons

FOUR Seasons fill the measure of the year ;
　　　There are four seasons in the mind of man :
He has his lusty Spring, when fancy clear
　　　Takes in all beauty with an easy span :
He has his Summer, when luxuriously
　　　Spring's honied cud of youthful thought he loves
To ruminate, and by such dreaming high
　　　Is nearest unto Heaven : quiet coves
His soul has in its Autumn, when his wings
　　　He furleth close ; contented so to look
On mists in idleness — to let fair things
　　　Pass by unheeded as a threshold brook.
He has his Winter too of pale misfeature,
Or else he would forego his mortal nature.

人的時令

四個季節循環成爲一年，
　　人的腦海也有四個時令，
他有他的歡愉的春天，
　　由幻想給攬來一切美景；
他有夏季，那時他愛咀嚼
　　華麗的春夢，春季的甜品，
他的夢想飛揚得這樣高，
　　使他最接近天庭；他的心
在秋天有了恬靜的港灣：
　　那時他折起翅膀，滿意於
懶懶望著霧色，滿懷冷淡
　　讓一切流去，像門前的小溪。
他也有蒼白而醜陋的冬令，
不然，他就喪失了人的本性。

1818年1-3月

To Homer

STANDING aloof in giant ignorance,
    Of thee I hear and of the Cyclades,
As one who sits ashore and longs perchance
    To visit dolphin-coral in deep seas.
So thou wast blind ! — but then the veil was rent ;
    For Jove uncurtain'd Heaven to let thee live,
And Neptune made for thee a spermy tent,
    And Pan made sing for thee his forest-hive ;
Aye, on the shores of darkness there is light,
    And precipices show untrodden green ;
There is a budding morrow in midnight, —
    There is a triple sight in blindness keen ;
Such seeing hadst thou, as it once befel
To Dian, Queen of Earth, and Heaven, and Hell.

致荷馬

孤獨的，被巨大的無知所包圍，
　　我耳聞到你和狄洛斯群島，*
正如一個岸上人，看到海水，
　　或想探視海豚所居的珊瑚礁。
誰說你是盲人！── 不，因爲約甫**
　　拉開了天帷讓你進去卜居，
海神爲你支起水泡的帳幕，
　　牧神讓蜜蜂給你唱著歌曲。
啊，黑暗底邊沿豈不是光亮！
　　懸崖上現出人跡不到的靑綠，
子夜裏有含苞待放的晨光，
　　盲人的眼睛也另有一種視力。
你就具有這種視覺，像是月神：
她主宰著人間、地獄、和天庭。

1818年

---

* 　狄洛斯（Delos）群島或賽克萊狄斯群島，在愛琴海中，希臘神話指爲日神阿波羅誕生
　之地。
** 約甫，羅馬神話中的天空之神，相當於希臘神話的宙斯。

On Visiting the Tomb of Burns

THE town, the churchyard, and the setting sun,
　　The clouds, the trees, the rounded hills all seem,
Though beautiful, cold — strange — as in a dream,
I dreamed long ago, now new begun.
The short-lived paly Summer is but won
From Winter's ague, for one hour's gleam ;
Though sapphire-warm, their stars do never beam :
All is cold Beauty ; pain is never done :
For who has mind to relish, Minos-wise,
The Real of Beauty, free from that dead hue
Sickly imagination and sick pride
Cast wan upon it !　Burns !　with honour due
I oft have honour'd thee.　Great shadow ! hide
Thy face ; I sin against thy native skies.

訪彭斯墓*

這個小市鎮、這墓場、這圓山、
雲、樹木和夕陽，雖然美麗，
卻冰冷、陌生，彷彿我久已
夢見過的，現在重又夢見。
這樣短促而蒼白的夏天
彷彿只是冬之瘧疾的迴光，
這星星雖似藍玉，卻不閃亮，
一切美而冷；痛苦說不完：
因為啊，誰像敏諾斯，**能體會
美底實體，使它不致染上
虛弱的想像和可厭的虛榮
所投的暗影！　彭斯啊，我常常
敬重你。　隱去吧，偉大的陰靈！
我不該把你的家園責備。

1818年7月2日

* 彭斯（R. Burns, 1756—1796），蘇格蘭偉大的詩人。濟慈在訪問他的墳墓後，給弟弟
　托姆寫信說道：「我在一種奇怪的、半睡的心情下寫了這篇十四行詩。我不知道為什
　麼覺得那雲彩，那天空，那房子，都是違反希臘風和查理曼風的。」
** 敏諾斯是宙斯之子，因為論斷公正，死後封為地獄中的最高裁判。

To Ailsa Rock

HEARKEN, thou craggy ocean-pyramid,
  Give answer by thy voice — the sea-fowls' screams !
    When were thy shoulders mantled in huge streams ?
When from the sun was thy broad forehead hid ?
How long is't since the mighty Power bid
  Thee heave to airy sleep from fathom dreams —
  Sleep in the lap of thunder or sunbeams —
Or when grey clouds are thy cold coverlid !
Thou answer'st not ; for thou art dead asleep.
  Thy life is but two dead eternities,
The last in air, the former in the deep !
  First with the whales, last with the eagle-skies !
Drown'd wast thou till an earthquake made thee steep,
  Another cannot wake thy giant size !

訪阿麗沙巉岩

喂！你海洋上巉岩的金字塔，
　　瀑布幾時披上了你的肩膀？
　　你的額角幾時躲開了太陽？
請以海鷗的叫喊給我回答！
有力的造物主幾時讓你離開
　　海底的夢，把你舉上天空的
　　睡眠，在雷電或陽光的懷裏，
而白雲成了你寒冷的被蓋？
啊，你不答；因為你在睡眠。
　　你一生是兩個死寂的永恆：
一端伴著鯨魚，在海底深淵；
　　另一端在巨鷹翱翔的空中！
除非是地震把你拔上青天，
　　誰能將你巨大的軀體喚醒！

1818年7月10日

Written in the Cottage where Burns was born

THIS mortal body of a thousand days
    Now fills, O Burns, a space in thine own room,
Where thou didst dream alone on budded bays,
Happy and thoughtless of thy day of doom !
My pulse is warm with thine own Barley-bree,
My head is light with pledging a great soul,
My eyes are wandering, and I cannot see,
Fancy is dead and drunken at its goal ;
Yet can I stamp my foot upon thy floor,
Yet can I ope thy window-sash to find
The meadow thou hast tramped o' er and o' er, —
Yet can I think of thee till thought is blind, —
Yet can I gulp a bumper to thy name, —
O smile among the shades, for this is fame !

寫於彭斯誕生的村屋

這個壽命不及千日的軀體，
彭斯啊，現在站進了你的小屋，
你曾在這裏獨自夢想詩譽，
從不知道命運怎樣將你擺布。
你的麥汁使的血液沸騰，
我不禁陶醉了，我頭暈目眩，
因為偉大的靈魂在和我對飲：
終於，幻想沉醉地到達終點。
儘管如此，我還能在你的房間
踱來踱去，還能打開窗戶
看到你所常常行經的草原，
還能想到你，並且飲酒祝福
你的名字 —— 哦，彭斯，在陰界裏
微笑吧，因為這就是人的聲譽。

To Sleep

O SOFT embalmer of the still midnight !
    Shutting, with careful fingers and benign,
Our gloom-pleased eyes, embower'd from the light,
    Enshaded in forgetfulness divine ;
O soothest Sleep ! if so it please thee, close,
    In midst of this thine hymn, my willing eyes,
Or wait the amen, ere thy poppy throws
    Around my bed its lulling charities ;
    Then save me, or the passed day will shine
Upon my pillow, breeding many woes ;
    Save me from curious conscience, that still lords
Its strength for darkness, burrowing like a mole ;
    Turn the key deftly in the oiled wards,
And seal the hushed casket of my soul.

詠睡眠

哦，午夜的溫馨的安慰者，
　　請用善意的手，小心地合上
這愛幽暗的眼睛，使它躲過
　　光亮，躲進了聖潔的遺忘。
甜蜜的睡眠啊！你的這頌禱，
　　如果你願意，盡可不必唱完
就閉上我的眼，或者直等到
　　「阿們」，再把罌粟灑在我床邊。

　　搭救我吧；否則，逝去的太陽
就會照在枕上，滋生憂鬱；
　　快讓我擺脫開這好奇的心，
它像鼴鼠，最會向黑暗裏鑽；
　　請輕輕鎖上這滑潤的牢門，
啊，請封閉我這寂靜的靈棺。

1819年4月

On Fame

FAME, like a wayward girl, will still be coy
        To those who woo her with too slavish knees,
But makes surrender to some thoughtless boy,
        And dotes the more upon a heart at ease ;
She is a Gipsy will not speak to those
        Who have not learnt to be content without her ;
A Jilt, whose ear was never whisper'd close,
        Who thinks they scandal her who talk about her ;
A very Gipsy is she, Nilus-born,
        Sister-in-law to jealous Potiphar ;
Ye love-sick Bards ! repay her scorn for scorn ;
        Ye Artists lovelorn ! madmen that ye are !
Make your best bow to her and bid adieu,
Then, if she likes it, she will follow you.

詠聲名

聲名像個野性女兒，但仍然
　　對朝她奴顏婢膝的人畏縮，
輕浮的小伙子討她喜歡，
　　淡漠的心才叫她難分難捨；
她是個吉卜賽，不喜歡答理
　　那沒有她就活不愜意的人，
而且朝三暮四：別跟她低語，
　　誰談到她；必然會使她心懷怨恨；
啊，她這吉卜賽，生在奈拉斯*，
　　簡直是嫉妒的波提乏**的妻子，
單戀的詩人！你該報她以蔑視；
　　藝術家啊！何必爲她癲狂、迷醉！
請對她翩然一躬，說聲再會，
如果她高興，自會把你追隨。

1819年4月30日

---

*　奈拉斯，尼羅河的古稱。
**　《舊約》〈創世紀〉中記載，波提乏的妻子引誘奴僕約瑟不成，惱羞成怒，反誣約
　　瑟，使波提乏把他關進監獄。

On Fame

"You cannot eat your cake and have it too." — *Proverb.*

HOW fever'd is the man, who cannot look
  Upon his mortal days with temperate blood,
Who vexes all the leaves of his life's book,
  And robs his fair name of its maidenhood ;
It is as if the rose should pluck herself,
  Or the ripe plum finger its misty bloom,
As if a Naiad, like a meddling elf,
  Should darken her pure grot with muddy gloom ;
But the rose leaves herself upon the briar,
  For winds to kiss and grateful bees to feed,
And the ripe plum still wears its dim attire ;
  The undisturbed lake has crystal space ;
  Why then should man, teasing the world for grace,
Spoil his salvation for a fierce miscreed ?

詠聲名

你不能又吃糕，又有糕。 ── 諺語

多蠢的人！不能冷靜地對待
　他有限的時日，而必得干擾
生命這本書，把每一頁塗壞，
　從而剝奪了他美名的貞操；
這好像是玫瑰把自己摘取，
　李樹搖落了全身花朵的霧，
又像水中的女神頑皮多事，
　用泥污攪渾她純淨的洞府；
可是啊，玫瑰豈不仍在枝上，
　等風兒親吻，等蜜蜂來啜飲？
李樹仍舊披著暗紅的衣裳，
　湖面上也依然鋪展著水晶：
　那麼，何以急於想得救的人
倒信仰一個殘酷邪異的神？

1819年4月30日

"If by dull rhymes our English must be chain'd"

IF by dull rhymes our English must be chain'd,
    And, like Andromeda, the Sonnet sweet
Fetter'd, in spite of pained loveliness ;
Let us find out, if we must be constrain'd,
    Sandals more interwoven and complete
To fit the naked foot of poesy ;
Let us inspect the lyre, and weigh the stress
Of every chord, and see what may be gain'd
    By ear industrious, and attention meet ;
Misers of sound and syllable, no less
Than Midas of his coinage, let us be
    Jealous of dead leaves in the bay wreath crown ;
So, if we may not let the Muse be free,
    She will be bound with garlands of her own.

「假如英詩」*

假如英詩必須被呆板的韻式
　　束縛住，而甜蜜的十四行
不管受多少苦，也得戴上鎖鍊；
假如我們必須受一種節制，
　　那就讓我們給詩底赤腳穿上
編得更精細的草鞋，處處合宜。
讓我們把豎琴檢察一下，彈彈
每根弦的重音，不斷地嘗試，
　　看怎樣能找出最適切的音響。
讓我們像米達斯**吝惜金錢
那樣地珍惜聲韻吧，要精於
　　使用每片枯葉去編織桂冠；
這樣啊，假如繆斯必須受制，
　　至少是受制於她自己的花環。

1819年2－7月

---

   * 本詩韻式較複雜，為12312431234545。這似乎是為了證明其中提出的主張。
** 米達斯，古代弗里吉亞傳說中的國王，他求神使他觸到的一切都變為黃金，這個願心
　　雖然實現，他卻不再能吃東西了。

"The day is gone"

THE day is gone, and all its sweets are gone !
   Sweet voice, sweet lips, soft hand, and softer breast,
Warm breath, light whisper, tender semi-tone,
   Bright eyes, accomplish'd shape, and lang'rous waist !
Faded the flower and all its budded charms,
   Faded the sight of beauty from my eyes,
Faded the shape of beauty from my arms,
   Faded the voice, warmth, whiteness, paradise —
Vanish'd unseasonably at shut of eve,
   When the dusk holiday — or holinight
Of fragrant-curtain'd love begins to weave
   The woof of darkness thick, for hid delight ;
But, as I've read love's missal through to-day,
He'll let me sleep, seeing I fast and pray.

「白天逝去了」*

白天逝去了，它的樂趣也都失去！
　　柔嫩的手，更柔的胸，嬌音和紅唇，
溫馨的呼吸，多情的、如夢的低語，
　　明眸，豐盈的體態，細軟的腰身！
一切違時地消逝了，唉，當黃昏 ——
　　那愛情的夜晚，那幽暗的節日
爲了以香帷遮住祕密的歡情，
　　正開始把昏黑的夜幕密密編織；
而這時，一朵鮮花，她飽含的魅力
　　枯萎了，我眼前的麗影無踪；
枯萎了，我懷抱著的美底形體；
　　枯萎了，聲音、溫暖、皎潔和天庭 ——
但今天我旣已讀過愛情底聖書，
而又齋戒、祈禱過，它該讓我睡熟。

1819年10－12月

---

* 本詩和以後兩首都是寫給詩人的戀人范妮‧勃朗的。

"I cry your mercy — pity — love !"

I CRY your mercy — pity — love ! — aye, love !
    Merciful love that tantalises not,
One-thoughted, never-wandering, guileless love,
    Unmask'd, and being seen — without a blot !
O ! let me have thee whole, — all — all — be mine !
    That shape, that fairness, that sweet minor zest
Of love, your kiss, — those hands, those eyes divine,
    That warm, white, lucent, million-pleasured breast, —
Yourself — your soul — in pity give me all,
    Withhold no atom's atom or I die,
Or living on, perhaps, your wretched thrall,
    Forget, in the mist of idle misery,
Life's purposes, — the palate of my mind
Losing its gust, and my ambition blind !

「我求你的仁慈」

我懇求你的仁慈，憐憫，愛情！
　　啊，我要仁慈的愛情，從不誆騙；
要它無邪、專一、別無二心，
　　坦開了胸懷 —— 沒一點污斑！
哦，讓我整個擁有你，整個的！
　　那身姿、美色、眼、手、和你的吻 ——
一種甜蜜而次要的愛慾，——
　　以及那胸脯：玉潔、溫暖、透明、
儲有萬千樂趣；啊，統統給我：
　　你，和你的靈魂，別留一星星；
否則我會死；或者，也許活著，
　　成為你悲慘的奴隸，被投進
暗淡苦惱的迷霧裏，失去了
生活的情趣、雄心和目標！

1819年10－12月

Written on a Blank Page in Skakespeare's Poems, facing A Lover's Complaint

B RIGHT star ! would I were steadfast as thou art —
　　　Not in lone splendour hung aloft the night,
And watching, with eternal lids apart,
　　　Like Nature's patient, sleepless Eremite,
The moving waters at their priestlike task
　　　Of pure ablution round earth's human shores,
Or gazing on the new soft fallen mask
　　　Of snow upon the mountains and the moors —
No — yet still steadfast, still unchangeable,
　　　Pillow'd upon my fair love's ripening breast,
To feel for ever its soft fall and swell,
　　　Awake for ever in a sweet unrest,
Still, still to hear her tender-taken breath,
And so live ever — or else swoon to death.

「燦爛的星」 *

燦爛的星！我祈求像你那樣堅定 ──
　　但我不願意高懸夜空，獨自
輝映，並且永恆地睜著眼睛，
　　像自然間耐心的、不眠的隱士，
不斷望著海濤，那大地的神父，
　　用聖水沖洗人所卜居的岸沿，
或者注視飄飛的白雪，像面幕，
　　燦爛、輕盈、覆蓋著窪地和高山 ──
啊，不， ── 我只願堅定不移地
　　以頭枕在愛人酥軟的胸脯上，
永遠感到它舒緩的降落、升起；
　　而醒來，心裏充滿甜蜜的激蕩，
不斷、不斷聽著她細膩的呼吸，
　　就這樣活著 ── 或昏迷地死去。

1820年9月28日

---

* 這是濟慈的最後一首詩，寫於自英國赴義大利的海船上。

Sleep and Poetry

"*As I lay in my bed slepe full unmete*

Was unto me, but why that I ne might

Rest I ne wist, for there n'as erthly wight

[As I suppose] had more of hertis ese

Than I, for I n'ad sicknesse nor disese."

CHAUCER.

WHAT is more gentle than a wind in summer?
 What is more soothing than the pretty hummer
That stays one moment in an open flower,
And buzzes cheerily from bower to bower ?
What is more tranquil than a musk-rose blowing
In a green island, far from all men's knowing ?
More healthful than the leafiness of dales ?
More secret than a nest of nightingales ?
More serene than Cordelia's countenance ?
More full of visions than a high romance ?   10
What, but thee Sleep ?   Soft closer of our eyes !
Low murmurer of tender lullabies !
Light hoverer around our happy pillows !
Wreather of poppy buds, and weeping willows !
Silent entangler of a beauty's tresses !

睡與詩

我躺在床上時，睡眠總是不肯
來到我身邊，我不知道為什麼
不能安息，因為（據我推測）
世上有誰比我更心神平靜？
因為我既無疾苦，也無病症。

—— 喬叟

有什麼比夏天的風更溫存？
有什麼比嚶嚶的蜜蜂更怡情？
它在盛開的花間只停留一瞬，
又快樂地從涼蔭飛到涼蔭。
什麼能靜似麝香薔薇的開放，
遠離人的踪跡，在青綠的島上？
什麼比山谷的蔥綠更爽人身體？
或者比夜鶯的巢更深藏、隱秘？
或者比考德莉亞*的面容更安詳？
比騎士小說更充滿了幻象？
什麼？除了你，睡眠？　啊，輕輕閉合
我們眼睛的、催眠曲的低唱者！
你在快樂的枕上輕輕盤旋，
把罌粟花蕾和柳枝編成花環；
你悄悄撩亂了美人的髮辮，

* 莎士比亞悲劇《李耳王》中的女主人公。

Most happy listener ! when the morning blesses

Thee for enlivening all the cheerful eyes

That glance so brightly at the new sun-rise.

But what is higher beyond thought than thee ?

Fresher than berries of a mountain tree ?   20

More strange, more beautiful, more smooth, more regal,

Than wings of swans, than doves, than dim-seen eagle ?

What is it ?   And to what shall I compare it ?

It has a glory, and nought else can share it :

The thought thereof is awful, sweet, and holy,

Chacing away all worldliness and folly ;

Coming sometimes like fearful claps of thunder,

Or the low rumblings earth's regions under ;

And sometimes like a gentle whispering

Of all the secrets of some wond'rous thing   30

That breathes about us in the vacant air ;

So that we look around with prying stare,

Perhaps to see shapes of light, aerial lymning,

And catch soft floatings from a faint-heard hymning ;

To see the laurel wreath, on high suspended,

That is to crown our name when life is ended.

Sometimes it gives a glory to the voice,

And from the heart up-springs, rejoice ! rejoice !

Sounds which will reach the Framer of all things,

又快樂地傾聽早晨向你問安：
它祝福你，因爲你教眼睛靈活，
使它們能對旭日明亮地閃爍。

但是，什麼比你更崇高得無限？
什麼比山樹上的果實更新鮮？
比天鵝的翅、鴿子、和高飛的鷹，
更莊嚴、美麗、奇異而寧靜？
那是什麼？　我將怎樣來比喻？
它有一種榮耀，誰也不能企及：
一想到它，便覺敬畏、甜蜜、神聖，
驅散了一切凡俗和愚蠢；
它來時有如可怕的雷鳴，
或是大地底層的低沉的轟隆；
有時候，也像溫柔的低語
訴說一些奇異事物的秘密；
這秘密就隱約在我們周身，
使我們不由得放眼搜尋，
想看到光中之形，空中之影，
從聽不清的讚詩中掠得清音；
想看見月桂花冠懸在半空，
等生命告終，就罩上我們的姓名。
又有時候，它躍自我們的心窩，
給聲音添上榮耀：歡樂吧！歡樂！
這聲音將直達造物主那裏，

And die away in ardent mutterings.   40

No one who once the glorious sun has seen,
And all the clouds, and felt his bosom clean
For his great Maker's presence, but must know
What 'tis I mean, and feel his being glow :
Therefore no insult will I give his spirit,
By telling what he sees from native merit.

O Poesy ! for thee I hold my pen
That am not yet a glorious denizen
Of thy wide heaven — Should I rather kneel
Upon some mountain-top until I feel   50
A glowing splendour round about me hung,
And echo back the voice of thine own tongue ?
O Poesy! for thee I grasp my pen
That am not yet a glorious denizen
Of thy wide heaven ; yet, to my ardent prayer,
Yield from thy sanctuary some clear air,
Smoothed for intoxication by the breath
Of flowering bays, that I may die a death
Of luxury, and my young spirit follow
The morning sun-beams to the great Apollo   60
Like a fresh sacrifice ; or, if I can bear
The o'erwhelming sweets, 'twill bring to me the fair

在熱烈的喃喃中裊裊逝去。

只要誰見過一次太陽的光輝
和雲彩，感到自己無所愧對
偉大的造物主，他必然知道
我說的是什麼，從而全心歡躍：
因此，我不會使他精神不快，
把他原本知道的再講出來。

哦，詩歌！我為你拿起了筆，
雖然我，在你廣大的天空裏
還不是光榮的居民 —— 我可要
跪在某座山頂上，直等我感到
我周身全是燦爛的榮光，
並且把你的歌聲不斷迴蕩？
哦，詩歌！我為你拿起了筆，
雖然我，在你廣大的天空裏
還不是光榮的居民；但懇求你
從你那聖殿吹來清新的空氣，
為了迷人，再融以月桂的芬芳，
使我能有一次奢靡的死亡；
那麼，我青春的幽靈將會跟蹤
晨曦的光線，像新鮮的祭品，
直達偉大的阿波羅；不然，我如若
竟受得住這美感，它必能使我

Visions of all places : a bowery nook

Will be elysium — an eternal book

Whence I may copy many a lovely saying

About the leaves, and flowers — about the playing

Of nymphs in woods, and fountains ; and the shade

Keeping a silence round a sleeping maid ;

And many a verse from so strange influence

That we must ever wonder how, and whence   70

It came.   Also imaginings will hover

Round my fire-side, and haply there discover

Vistas of solemn beauty, where I'd wander

In happy silence, like the clear Meander

Through its lone vales ; and where I found a spot

Of awfuller shade, or an enchanted grot,

Or a green hill o'erspread with chequered dress

Of flowers, and fearful from its loveliness,

Write on my tablets all that was permitted,

All that was for our human senses fitted.   80

Then the events of this wide world I'd seize

Like a strong giant, and my spirit teaze

Till at its shoulders it should proudly see

Wings to find out an immortality.

看到種種仙境：一角樹蔭處
就是一個樂園，一本永恆的書：
從那裏可以抄出很多雋語，
講著葉和花 —— 講著林中的仙女
怎樣和泉水嬉戲，以及那樹蔭
怎樣給沉睡的少女灑一片靜；
還可以從那裏抄出很多詩句：
我們必然驚愕，它們如此奇異，
不知來自何方。　而且很多幻想
會在我爐邊繚繞，我或許能碰上
蕭穆的美底幻景：我將喜於
在那裏靜靜遊蕩，像清澈的
米安得*流過幽谷；只要我發現
迷人的岩洞，或更陰森的林間，
或是青山以鮮花織的錦衣
鋪在身上，可愛得令人畏懼，
我就將在我的石板上書寫
可寫的、賦與人的感官的一切。
那時，我將像巨人一樣抓緊
這大千世界的一切，無限歡欣，
直到驕傲地看見在我肩上
生出能夠飛往永恆的翅膀。

＊　冥府中的河水，以曲折著稱。

Stop and consider ! life is but a day ;
A fragile dew-drop on its perilous way
From a tree's summit ; a poor Indian's sleep
While his boat hastens to the monstrous steep
Of Montmorenci.   Why so sad a moan ?
Life is the rose's hope while yet unblown ;   90
The reading of an ever-changing tale ;
The light uplifting of a maiden's veil ;
A pigeon tumbling in clear summer air ;
A laughing school-boy, without grief or care,
Riding the springy branches of an elm.

O for ten years, that I may overwhelm
Myself in poesy ; so I may do the deed
That my own soul has to itself decreed.
Then will I pass the countries that I see
In long perspective, and continually   100
Taste their pure fountains.   First the realm I'll pass
Of Flora, and old Pan : sleep in the grass,
Feed upon apples red, and strawberries,
And choose each pleasure that my fancy sees ;
Catch the white-handed nymphs in shady places,
To woo sweet kisses from averted faces, —
Play with their fingers, touch their shoulders white
Into a pretty shrinking with a bite

靜靜想想吧！生命不過是瞬息；
是從樹頂落下的渺小的露滴
所走的險徑；是印度人的睡眠，
正當他的船衝向凶險的懸崖，
在芒莫倫西。　但何必如此哀傷？
生命是沒開的玫瑰的希望；
是同一故事永遠不同的誦讀；
是少女的面紗的輕輕揭露；
是一隻鴿子翻飛在清朗的夏空；
是一個不知憂愁的小學童
騎著一條有彈性的榆樹枝。

啊，但願給我十年，使我得以
浸沉在詩歌裏；那我就要去
從事我的心靈所擬定的業迹。
我將到我曾從遠方瞻望的
國度去遊歷，不斷品嘗那兒的
清純的甘泉。　首先，我要去遊逛
花神和老獵神的國度：睡在草上，
以鮮紅的蘋果和楊梅充飢，
任憑幻想的指引去盡情遊戲；
我要在林蔭裏捕捉玉腕的女神，
從閃躲的面頰追求甜蜜的吻，──
摩弄她們的手指，觸摸潔白的臂膀，
以致她們嫵媚地一縮，狠狠地

As hard as lips can make it : till agreed,
A lovely tale of human life we'll read.   110
And one will teach a tame dove how it best
May fan the cool air gently o'er my rest ;
Another, bending o'er her nimble tread,
Will set a green robe floating round her head,
And still will dance with ever varied ease,
Smiling upon the flowers and the trees :
Another will entice me on, and on
Through almond blossoms and rich cinnamon ;
Till in the bosom of a leafy world
We rest in silence, like two gems upcurl'd   120
In the recesses of a pearly shell.

And can I ever bid these joys farewell ?
Yes, I must pass them for a nobler life,
Where I may find the agonies, the strife
Of human hearts : for lo ! I see afar,
O'er sailing the blue cragginess, a car
And steeds with streamy manes — the charioteer
Looks out upon the winds with glorious fear :
And now the numerous tramplings quiver lightly
Along a huge cloud's ridge ; and now with sprightly   130
Wheel downward come they into fresher skies,
Tipt round with silver from the sun's bright eyes.

用嘴唇來咬我：終於我們同意
一起讀一篇旖旎的人生故事。
有一個仙女會敎鴿子輕輕地
爲安睡的我搧動淸涼的空氣；
另一個屈身停下輕捷的步履，
整一整綠色的飄揚的紗衣：
接著仍舊對花和樹木微笑，
帶著瞬息萬變的情致舞蹈；
另一個招著手，悄悄引我行經
杏花叢和芬芳的肉桂樹林，
最後走進一個綠葉世界的懷抱，
我們靜靜地歇下來，像貝殼
所深藏的兩顆眞珠，伏在一起。

啊，我怎能拋下這許多樂趣？
是的，我必須捨棄它們去尋找
更崇高的生活：從而看到
人心的痛苦和衝突；因爲，哦！
我看見遠天上，一駕飛速的馬車
馳過崎嶇的藍色 —— 駕車的人
帶著輝煌的恐懼探望著風：
一會兒在一片巨雲的峰頂
輕顫地踏了過去，一會兒他們
又敏捷地駛進另一片靑天，
車輪被太陽的光輝染成銀環。

Still downward with capacious whirl they glide ;
And now I see them on a green-hill's side
In breezy rest among the nodding stalks.
The charioteer with wond'rous gesture talks
To the trees and mountains ; and there soon appear
Shapes of delight, of mystery, and fear,
Passing along before a dusky space
Made by some mighty oaks : as they would chase   140
Some ever-fleeting music on they sweep.
Lo ! how they murmur, laugh, and smile, and weep :
Some with upholden hand and mouth severe ;
Some with their faces muffled to the ear
Between their arms ; some, clear in youthful bloom,
Go glad and smilingly athwart the gloom ;
Some looking back, and some with upward gaze ;
Yes, thousands in a thousand different ways
Flit onward — now a lovely wreath of girls
Dancing their sleek hair into tangled curls ;   150
And now broad wings.   Most awfully intent
The driver of those steeds is forward bent,
And seems to listen : O that I might know
All that he writes with such a hurrying glow.

The visions all are fled — the car is fled
Into the light of heaven, and in their stead

在下坡時，他們更快地奔跑；
忽而我見他們在綠色的山腳
歇了下來；在搖擺的花梗中間，
駕車者以奇異的手勢對山巒
和樹木談話；轉瞬間，在那裏
出現了喜悅、神秘、恐懼底形體，
它們在一片橡樹林的陰影前
迅速掠過，彷彿它們是在追趕
飄飛的樂音。哦！看它們正怎樣
低聲喃喃，鬨笑，喜悅，或悲傷：
有的舉起手來，嘴角嚴肅；
有的以雙手把面孔遮住
直遮到耳朵；有的青春盛年，
欣喜而微笑地穿過了幽暗；
有的頻頻回顧；有的抬頭仰視；
是的，千萬形體以千萬種方式
掠過去 ── 一會兒，可愛的一圈
小姑娘，把光潤的頭髮跳得紛亂；
又一會伸出翅膀。　趕馬的車夫
身子向前傾側，凝神而嚴肅
彷彿他在諦聽：哦，我多想知悉
他在一閃爍間記下的東西。

幻象飛散了 ── 車駕已消失
在天庭的光輝裏，接著來的是

A sense of real things comes doubly strong,

And, like a muddy stream, would bear along

My soul to nothingness : but I will strive

Against all doubtings, and will keep alive 160

The thought of that same chariot, and the strange

Journey it went.

    Is there so small a range

In the present strength of manhood, that the high

Imagination cannot freely fly

As she was wont of old ? prepare her steeds,

Paw up against the light, and do strange deeds

Upon the clouds ? Has she not shown us all ?

From the clear space of ether, to the small

Breath of new buds unfolding ? From the meaning

Of Jove's large eye-brow, to the tender greening 170

Of April meadows ? Here her altar shone,

E'en in this isle ; and who could paragon

The fervid choir that lifted up a noise

Of harmony, to where it aye will poise

Its mighty self of convoluting sound,

Huge as a planet, and like that roll round,

Eternally around a dizzy void ?

Ay, in those days the Muses were nigh cloy'd

更頑強的現實事物的感覺 ——
它像是渾濁的水流，要拖曳
我的心靈直抵虛無：但我卻要
排除一切疑慮，只清晰地記牢
那駕車，和它所走的奇異旅程。

難道如今，人的精神能力已經
如此微弱有限，崇高的幻想
再也不能像自己以往那樣
自由地翱翔？再也不能備好坐騎，
向光明邁出，作出神奇的業迹
在雲端上？　難道我們不曾見她*
自澄澈的大氣以至初開的花
所發的芬芳裏？　自約甫的蹙額
以至四月草原的一片綠色？
即使在這個島上，她的神壇
也曾輝煌；誰曾勝過這個合唱班？**
它唱過熱烈而和諧的歌，這歌聲
直達天宇，就在那兒永遠形成
巨大的迴旋之音，有如行星；
有如行星環繞著眩人的真空
永恆地運轉。啊，在過去那時日，
繆斯們豈非如此載滿了榮譽？

* 　「她」指「崇高的幻想」。
** 　指喬叟及伊利莎白時代的詩人們。

With honors ; nor had any other care
Than to sing out and sooth their wavy hair.   180

Could all this be forgotten ?   Yes, a schism
Nurtured by foppery and barbarism,
Made great Apollo blush for this his land.
Men were thought wise who could not understand
His glories : with a puling infant's force
They sway'd about upon a rocking horse,
And thought it Pegasus.   Ah dismal soul'd !
The winds of heaven blew, the ocean roll'd
Its gathering waves — ye felt it not.   The blue
Bared its eternal bosom, and the dew   190
Of summer nights collected still to make
The morning precious : beauty was awake !
Why were ye not awake ?   But ye were dead
To things ye knew not of, — were closely wed
To musty laws lined out with wretched rule
And compass vile : so that ye taught a school
Of dolts to smooth, inlay, and clip, and fit,
Till, like the certain wands of Jacob's wit,

她們整日無所事事，除了高歌，
除了把她們的鬈髮輕輕撫摸。

難道這一切都遺忘了？　是的，
由盲昧主義和浮華所培育的
一個教派，*使阿波羅對這片領地
感到羞慚。　那不解他的榮耀的，
被認為智者：他們騎著一隻木馬，
使盡了稚弱的力氣搖動它，
當它是彼加斯。**噫，心靈多渺小！
天空的風在吹，凝聚的海濤
在滾轉 ── 你們卻不見。　蔚藍的天
坦露著永恆的胸懷，在夏晚
露水靜靜地凝聚，為了使清早
更為珍奇：美普遍地甦醒了！
何以你們總是不醒？　但你們
對你們不知的事物無動於衷，
只守著發霉的教條，又充塞以
邪惡的法規和鄙陋的戒律。
你們教一群愚人把詩句磨光、
切割、鑲配，使它們像雅各的魔枝***

* 　指違反伊利莎白詩歌傳統的十八世紀古典主義派。
** 　彼加斯，詩神所騎的神馬，靈感的象徵。
***《聖經》〈創世紀〉載：「雅各拿楊樹杏樹楓樹的嫩枝，剝皮，剝成紋理，使枝子露
　　出白的來，將剝了皮的枝子插在飲羊的水溝和水槽裏，對著羊，羊來喝的時候，牝牡
　　配合，羊對著枝子配合，就生下有紋理的、有點的、有斑的羊羔來。「雅各的魔枝」
　　就是指的這種樹枝。

Their verses tallied.   Easy was the task :
A thousand handicraftsmen wore the mask   200
Of Poesy.   Ill-fated, impious race !
That blasphemed the bright Lyrist to his face,
And did not know it, — no, they went about,
Holding a poor, decrepid standard out
Mark'd with most flimsy mottos, and in large
The name of one Boileau !
                    Oh ye whose charge
It is to hover round our pleasant hills!
Whose congregated majesty so fills
My boundly reverence, that I cannot trace
Your hallowed names, in this unholy place,   210
So near those common folk ; did not their shames
Affright you ?   Did our old lamenting Thames
Delight you ?   Did ye never cluster round
Delicious Avon, with a mournful sound,
And weep ?   Or did ye wholly bid adieu
To regions where no more the laurel grew ?
Or did ye stay to give a welcoming
To some lone spirits who could proudly sing
Their youth away, and die ?   'Twas even so :

配合起來。這工作真太容易：
成千工匠都戴上了詩底面具：
啊，倒霉的、邪惡的一族！　凌犯了
光輝的抒情詩人，卻還不知道！
不，他們到處招搖，舉著一支
破舊的、標以浮淺口號的旗幟，
上面寫著什麼波瓦洛*的姓名！

　　　哦，本該在我們可愛的山林中
翺翔的一群！　你們全體的莊嚴
早就充滿了我虔誠的心坎，
在這不潔的地方，離那些人太近，
我無法縷述你們崇高的姓名；
他們的無恥豈不使你們驚異？
我們古老的幽怨的泰晤士
豈不曾取悅你們？　你們豈不曾
聚在優美的愛萬，**同發出悲聲？
你們可是永別了這個地方，
因為桂花不再在這兒生長？
或是你們還留著，只等歡迎
一些孤寂的心靈把青春
驕傲地唱完，然後就死去？***
啊，正是這樣；但讓我別再提起

　＊　波瓦洛（Boileau, 1636—1711），法國古典主義的理論大師。
　＊＊　莎士比亞故鄉的河流。
＊＊＊　指詩人查特頓。

But let me think away those times of woe :   220
Now ' tis a fairer season ; ye have breathed
Rich benedictions o' er us ; ye have wreathed
Fresh garlands : for sweet music has been heard
In many places ; — some has been upstirr' d
From out its crystal dwelling in a lake,
By a swan' s ebon bill ; from a thick brake,
Nested and quiet in a valley mild,
Bubbles a pipe ; fine sounds are floating wild
About the earth : happy are ye and glad.

These things are doubtless : yet in truth we' ve had   230
Strange thunders from the potency of song ;
Mingled indeed with what is sweet and strong,
From majesty : but in clear truth the themes
Are ugly clubs, the Poets Polyphemes
Disturbing the grand sea.   A drainless shower
Of light is poesy ; ' tis the supreme of power ;
' Tis might half slumb' ring on its own right arm.
The very archings of her eye-lids charm

悲慘的時代吧：時光如此美好；

你們正給了我們熱切的祝禱；

你們已經編起新鮮的花環：

因爲，在很多地方都可以聽見

甜蜜的樂音； —— 啊，有的被天鵝的

黑喙喚醒了，*走出了湖中的

水晶的房屋；在安謐的谷中，

從那靜靜棲息的密樹叢

也漾出笛聲；大地正浮蕩著

悅耳的音調：你們歡欣而快樂。

這是無疑的；可是，我們也聽見

奇怪的雷鳴從詩底內部發散，

固然，由於不凡，那聲音也混有

美妙和雄渾的因素，但仍舊 ——

那些主題顯然是醜陋的棍棒，**

詩人波里菲姆***們把輝煌的海洋

攪亂了。　詩本是光之無盡竭的

灑落；詩是最崇高的神力，

支著自己的右手，半睡半醒。

---

* 　據推測：指華滋華斯。

** 　「棍棒」（clubs）一辭，以及隨後的一句，頗爲費解，因此有的校訂家以爲必有勘誤
　　處。這裏係照西林考特的版本及解釋譯出。

*** 波里菲姆是一個獨眼巨人，把漂流的攸利西斯拘留在他的岩洞裏，每日吃下他的兩個
　　夥伴。攸利西斯設計弄瞎他的眼睛，得以脫逃。這裏似指：詩人們也像波里菲姆一
　　樣，是巨人，有超人之力，但也和波里菲姆似地瞎了眼睛，無法善用其精力，只好以
　　棍棒（主題）把詩的（或人生的）海洋胡攪一通。

A thousand willing agents to obey,

And still she governs with the mildest sway :   240

But strength alone though of the Muses born

Is like a fallen angel : trees uptorn,

Darkness, and worms, and shrouds, and sepulchres

Delight it ; for it feeds upon the burrs,

And thorns of life ; forgetting the great end

Of poesy, that it should be a friend

To sooth the cares, and lift the thoughts of man.

    Yet I rejoice : a myrtle fairer than

E' er grew in Paphos, from the bitter weeds

Lifts its sweet head into the air, and feeds   250

A silent space with ever sprouting green.

All tenderest birds there find a pleasant screen,

Creep through the shade with jaunty fluttering,

Nibble the little cupped flowers and sing.

Then let us clear away the choaking thorns

From round its gentle stem ; let the young fawns,

Yeaned in after times, when we are flown,

Find a fresh sward beneath it, overgrown

只要她魅人的眼皮動一動，

千萬志願的使者就會來效力，

而她只以溫煦的王笏治理。

但單純的力，雖然是繆斯所生，

卻像墮落的天使：唯有黑暗、蛆蟲、

掘倒的樹木、祭壇和屍衣，

使它心歡；因爲它以生之荊棘

和粗糙的磨石爲滋養；*忘記了

詩該是人的朋友，它偉大的目標

是寬慰憂慮，提高人的情思。

　　可是我也歡欣：因爲從苦艾裏

生出了桃金孃，勝過帕弗斯**

有過的花，它正甜蜜地伸入空氣，

把新抽的綠喂給寂靜的空間。

小鳥都把它看作可愛的屏藩，

穿躍濃蔭中，搧動著翅膀，

一面啄食小蛊花，一面歌唱。

讓我們從它的嫩莖旁斬除

那窒息它的荊棘吧，讓年輕的鹿

（在我們飄逝後誕生的一群）

在它下面找到新鮮的草坪

*　　這以上所形容的可能是拜倫；濟慈雖然早年崇尚拜倫，但後者的充滿狂暴熱情的陰鬱
　　詩歌逐漸爲他所不喜。在以下一段中，他歌頌像漢特那樣的恬靜的詩作，以與此對
　　照。

**　帕弗斯，地名，美神維納斯的奉祀地。

119

With simple flowers : let there nothing be

More boisterous than a lover's bended knee ;   260

Nought more ungentle than the placid look

Of one who leans upon a closed book ;

Nought more untranquil than the grassy slopes

Between two hills.   All hail delightful hopes !

As she was wont, th' imagination

Into most lovely labyrinths will be gone,

And they shall be accounted poet kings

Who simply tell the most heart-easing things.

O may these joys be ripe before I die.

Will not some say that I presumptuously   270

Have spoken ? that from hastening disgrace

'Twere better far to hide my foolish face ?

That whining boyhood should with reverence bow

Ere the dread thunderbolt could reach ?   How !

If I do hide myself, it sure shall be

In the very fane, the light of Poesy :

If I do fall, at least I will be laid

Beneath the silence of a poplar shade ;

And over me the grass shall be smooth shaven ;

And there shall be a kind memorial graven.   280

But off Despondence ! miserable bane !

They should not know thee, who athirst to gain

和樸素的花吧：那兒會非常靜，
只能聽見戀人屈膝的聲音；
也沒有一點俗氣，除了有人
倚著合上的書本，滿面從容；
更沒有什麼比山坳間的草坡
更喧嘩。　啊，向美好的希望祝賀！
讓幻想，像她經常那樣，走到
許多最可愛的迷宮裏逍遙；
讓凡能說故事的，就成爲詩王，
只要他單純的事物使心靈舒暢。
但願我在死前收穫這些樂趣！

會不會有人說，我是在囈語？
是否認爲在恥辱臨頭以前，
我頂好藏起自己愚痴的臉？
埋怨的少年要想不遭雷擊，
最好恭敬地屈身？　啊，去它的！
如果我隱藏，我要把自己
藏在詩底廟堂，詩底靈光裏：
如果我倒下了，至少我要躺下
在白楊樹蔭的一片靜謐下；
我墓前的青草會修剪得整齊，
一塊紀念的石碑在那兒豎立。
啊，去吧，沮喪！卑鄙的毒素！
凡是每一刻都在渴望和追逐

A noble end, are thirsty every hour.

What though I am not wealthy in the dower

Of spanning wisdom ; though I do not know

The shiftings of the mighty winds that blow

Hither and thither all the changing thoughts

Of man : though no great minist' ring reason sorts

Out the dark mysteries of human souls

To clear conceiving : yet there ever rolls   290

A vast idea before me, and I glean

Therefrom my liberty ; thence too I' ve seen

The end and aim of Poesy.   ' Tis clear

As anything most true ; as that the year

Is made of the four seasons — manifest

As a large cross, some old cathedral's crest,

Lifted to the white clouds.   Therefore should I

Be but the essence of deformity,

A coward, did my very eye-lids wink

At speaking out what I have dared to think.   300

Ah ! rather let me like a madman run

Over some precipice ; let the hot sun

Melt my Dedalian wings, and drive me down

Convuls' d and headlong !   Stay ! an inward frown

Of conscience bids me be more calm awhile.

An ocean dim, sprinkled with many an isle,

崇高目的的人，不會嘗到你。
儘管上天沒有給我很多急智，
儘管我不能知道巨大的風
把人類變幻的思想向哪裏吹動；
儘管我沒有雄偉濟世的智力，
從而把人類靈魂的幽暗秘密
化為清楚的思惟：但在我面前
永遠波動著一個巨大的概念，
我從它得到自由；從而我也看出
詩底終極和目標。　它像真實之物
一樣清晰，像一年由四季更替 ——
像老教堂屋頂上的大十字
高聳入白雲那樣明顯。　所以，
若果我真是懦夫，有意歪曲，
在我說出我大膽想到的話時，
可曾眨一眨眼？啊，寧可像瘋子，
讓我衝下懸崖吧；寧可讓太陽
熔化我的狄德勒斯的翅膀，*
使我痙攣地向下跌落！　哦，打住！
內心告訴我，我何必如此激怒？
一片幽暗的海洋，許多海島，

---

* 據古代神話：狄德勒斯以蠟和羽毛製成翅膀，他的兒子插上這種翅膀飛翔，因為接近太
　陽而致溶化，落海而死。

Spreads awfully before me.   How much toil !

How many days ! what desperate turmoil !

Ere I can have explored its widenesses.

Ah, what a task! upon my bended knees,   310

1 could unsay those — no, impossible !

Impossible !

          For sweet relief I'll dwell

On humbler thoughts, and let this strange assay

Begun in gentleness die so away.

E'en now all tumult from my bosom fades :

I turn full hearted to the friendly aids

That smooth the path of honour ; brotherhood,

And friendliness the nurse of mutual good.

The hearty grasp that sends a pleasant sonnet

Into the brain ere one can think upon it ;   320

The silence when some rhymes are coming out ;

And when they're come, the very pleasant rout :

The message certain to be done to-morrow.

'Tis perhaps as well that it should be to borrow

Some precious book from out its snug retreat,

To cluster round it when we next shall meet.

Scarce can I scribble on ; for lovely airs

Are fluttering round the room like doves in pairs ;

Many delights of that glad day recalling,

When first my senses caught their tender falling.   330

可畏地展示在我眼前。　這需要
多少勞力、時間、掙扎和奔忙，
才能探知它一切遼闊的地方！
啊，多大的辛苦！　我儘可以屈身
否認已說過的話 ── 但怎麼行！
怎麼行！

　　　　　爲了稍稍鬆一口氣，
我要說些瑣事，讓這不像樣的
試作，以高雅始，卻如此告終。
現在，我的胸中已復歸平靜：
我整個的心期望友好的援助
給我鋪平光明正直的道路；
期望友善：彼此福利底保姆。
我期望衷心的握手給頭腦注入
一首優美的十四行，以及那種
使詩韻得以暢流的一片安靜；
還有，當詩吟成時，那可喜的會集：
必定送個信，明天一定聚齊。
或許還可以取一本珍愛的書，
等我們再會時，圍著它閱讀。
我不能寫下去了；啊，優美的音響
像成雙的鴿子在室內翱翔；
我憶起那可喜一日的歡樂，
那時我的感官初嘗它們的柔波。

And with these airs come forms of elegance
Stooping their shoulders o'er a horse's prance,
Careless, and grand — fingers soft and round
Parting luxuriant curls ; — and the swift bound
Of Bacchus from his chariot, when his eye
Made Ariadne's cheek look blushingly.
Thus I remember all the pleasant flow
Of words at opening a portfolio.

Things such as these are ever harbingers
To trains of peaceful images : the stirs   340
Of a swan's neck unseen among the rushes :
A linnet starting all about the bushes :
A butterfly, with golden wings broad parted,
Nestling a rose, convuls'd as though it smarted
With over pleasure — many, many more,
Might I indulge at large in all my store
Of luxuries : yet I must not forget
Sleep, quiet with his poppy coronet :
For what there may be worthy in these rhymes
I partly owe to him : and thus, the chimes   350
Of friendly voices had just given place
To as sweet a silence, when I 'gan retrace

這聲音使我想起那優美的畫：
一群人坐在馬車上，莊嚴、瀟灑，
因急馳而傾著身，── 柔潤的手指
分著光澤的鬢髮；── 巴克科斯*
從車上急跳下來，他的眼睛
直使阿里阿德涅的面頰泛紅。
正是這樣，每當我打開畫頁，
我記起歌聲的美妙的流瀉。

像這樣的事物永遠會引動
一串和煦的形象：天鵝的頸
隱蔽在蘆葦裏，輕輕搖曳；
一隻紅雀驚吵了樹叢裏的一切；
一隻蝴蝶，展著金色的雙翼，
停在玫瑰花上，彷彿由於狂喜
而痛楚地顫動；── 還有很多，很多，
我可以懷著樂趣細細講說。
但是啊，我怎能忘記那靜靜的
圍以罌粟花的睡眠：因為，這裏
假如我寫了什麼像樣的詩行，
都該部分地歸功於它：就這樣，
溫煦的樂聲被同樣甜蜜的靜謐
所替代，而我在臥榻上憩息，

---

* 巴克科斯，酒神。阿里阿德涅被棄後意圖自盡，他援救了她，娶她為妻。這裏在形容一
幅畫。

The pleasant day, upon a couch at ease.

It was a poet's house who keeps the keys

Of pleasure's temple.   Round about were hung

The glorious features of the bards who sung

In other ages — cold and sacred busts

Smiled at each other.   Happy he who trusts

To clear Futurity his darling fame !

Then there were fauns and satyrs taking aim   360

At swelling apples with a frisky leap

And reaching fingers, 'mid a luscious heap

Of vine-leaves.   Then there rose to view a fane

Of liny marble, and thereto a train

Of nymphs approaching fairly o'er the sward :

One, loveliest, holding her white hand toward

The dazzling sun-rise : two sisters sweet

Bending their graceful figures till they meet

Over the trippings of a little child :

And some are hearing, eagerly, the wild   370

Thrilling liquidity of dewy piping.

See, in another picture, nymphs are wiping

Cherishingly Diana's timorous limbs ; —

A fold of lawny mantle dabbling swims

開始追憶那愉快的一天。　那是
一個詩人的家，*其中有把鑰匙
爲我打開喜悅底廟堂。　在屋裏，
四壁懸掛著曾在過去的世紀
高歌過的詩人的光輝身影 ──
他們彼此微笑著，神聖而冷靜。
啊，快樂的人！能把珍貴的聲名
寄託給晴朗的未來！　在室中
還有牧神和林神拿箭對著
密密藤葉間的圓潤的蘋果，
只等射中時，一個跳縱，用手指
把果子接住。我還看到大理石
建築的廟宇，一群仙女正越過
草地向那裏走去。　其中有一個
最美的，以玉手指著耀目的旭日；
有兩姊妹彎下秀麗的身軀
從兩邊去扶一個跌倒的兒童；
有一些少女正在注意聆聽
笛聲的有似露珠的滾滾流動。
看啊，在另一幅畫裏，仙女們
正輕輕洗拭狄安娜**的手足；
在浴池邊，一迭細麻的衣服

＊　濟慈是住在李・漢特的家中寫成本篇詩的。自此至篇終，都在描寫漢特書室中的牆畫
　　和藝術裝飾品。
＊＊　狄安娜，月底女神。

At the bath's edge, and keeps a gentle motion
With the subsiding crystal : as when ocean
Heaves calmly its broad swelling smoothness o'er
Its rocky marge, and balances once more
The patient weeds ; that now unshent by foam
Feel all about their undulating home.   380

Sappho's meek head was there half smiling down
At nothing ; just as though the earnest frown
Of over thinking had that moment gone
From off her brow, and left her all alone.

Great Alfred's too, with anxious, pitying eyes,
As if he always listened to the sighs
Of the goaded world ; and Kosciusko's worn
By horrid suffrance — mightily forlorn.
Petrarch, outstepping from the shady green,
Starts at the sight of Laura ; nor can wean   390
His eyes from her sweet face.   Most happy they !
For over them was seen a free display
Of out-spread wings, and from between them shone
The face of Poesy: from off her throne
She overlook'd things that I scarce could tell.
The very sense of where I was might well
Keep Sleep aloof : but more than that there came

浮一角在水裏，隨著晶瑩的蕩漾
輕輕地顫動：好像是海洋
在石岸上緩緩湧來了波濤，
使耐心的野草又一次飄搖；
而現在，旣然泡沫不來推聳，
草兒又在波動著尋求平衡。

莎弗和藹的面容對著空間
淡淡微笑，彷彿那一頃刻間
深思底皺眉剛剛離開了
她的前額，她又爲寂寞所圍繞。

還有偉大的阿弗瑞德，露著
焦灼而憐憫的眼神，像在聽著
世界的嘆息；還有克蘇斯珂的
痛苦而憔悴的臉 —— 異常悲悽。
彼特拉克從樹蔭裏走出來
看到勞拉，不勝驚羨；竟移不開
注意她的眼睛。　啊，他們多快樂！
因爲在他們肩上，自由地張著
一對翅膀，而詩底燦爛光輝
閃耀在他們之間：我又怎能描繪
她從她的寶座所看到的景象！
只要我意識到我處在的地方，
睡眠就會躲開；更何況，在我內心

Thought after thought to nourish up the flame
Within my breast ; so that the morning light
Surprised me even from a sleepless night ;   400
And up I rose refresh'd, and glad, and gay,
Resolving to begin that very day
These lines ; and howsoever they be done,
I leave them as a father does his son.

不斷的思緒使感情燒個不停；

因此我一夜未眠，但我仍然

爲晨光所驚醒，我起來，新鮮、

愉快而興奮，當天就決定了

寫下這些詩句，無論好與不好，

那只有隨它們去吧，正好像

作父親的放任他的孩子一樣。

1816年

附記：本詩最初的40行，解釋了「睡」與「詩」兩種意境，並將未醒的精神與覺醒的詩的精
神作了對比。自第85行（「靜靜想想吧」）至161行，濟慈寫出詩歌在他心目中所經歷
的階段，也就是列出他自己的發展過程。122—161行似在表示「（一）只有在同情地
理解人性以後，人才能與自然交感不隔並獲知其秘密的美；對自然與人生的理解是互
通的，相互作用的；（二）認識了自然所顯示的理想以後，惡濁的生活現實更顯得尖
銳而不可忍受，要不是有幻想——它使詩人心中的理想得以不死，使他免致絕望——
支持的話」（西林考特）。自162起的五十行，寫出詩人對當代詩壇的不滿並對十八世
紀的古典主義傾向提出尖刻的批評，這批評曾引起拜倫等人的反擊。這五十行之後，
可能是致伊利莎白時代的詩人們，並提出當前的歡愉景色。此後大致縷述詩人的信念
和願心。最後的六十餘行列舉漢特書室的藝術陳設。——譯者。

Ode to a Nightingale

1

M Y heart aches, and a drowsy numbness pains
My sense, as though of hemlock I had drunk,
Or emptied some dull opiate to the drains
One minute past, and Lethe-wards had sunk :
'Tis not through envy of thy happy lot,
But being too happy in thine happiness, —
That thou, light-winged Dryad of the trees,
In some melodious plot
Of beechen green, and shadows numberless,
Singest of summer in full-throated ease.

2

O, for a draught of vintage ! that hath been
Cool'd a long age in the deep-delved earth,
Tasting of Flora and the country green,
Dance, and Provençal song, and sunburnt mirth !
O for a beaker full of the warm South,
Full of the true, the blushful Hippocrene,

夜鶯頌

1

我的心在痛，困睏和麻木
　　刺進了感官，有如飲過毒鴆，
又像是剛剛把鴉片吞服，
　　於是向著列斯*忘川下沉：
並不是我嫉妒你的好運，
　　而是你的快樂使我太歡欣 ——
　　　　因為在林間嘹喨的天地裏，
　　　　　　你啊，輕翅的仙靈，
你躲進山毛櫸的蔥綠和蔭影，
　　　　放開了歌喉，歌唱著夏季。

2

唉，要是有一口酒！那冷藏
　　在地下多年的清醇飲料，
一嘗就令人想起綠色之邦，
　　想起花神，戀歌，陽光和舞蹈！
要是有一杯南國的溫暖
　　充滿了鮮紅的靈感之泉，

＊　列斯，冥府中的河，鬼魂飲了它便忘記前生的一切，亦譯「忘川」。

With beaded bubbles winking at the brim,
    And purple-stained mouth ;
That I might drink, and leave the world unseen,
    And with thee fade away into the forest dim :

3

Fade far away, dissolve, and quite forget
    What thou among the leaves hast never known,
The weariness, the fever, and the fret
    Here, where men sit and hear each other groan ;
Where palsy shakes a few, sad, last gray hairs,
    Where youth grows pale, and spectre-thin, and dies ;
        Where but to think is to be full of sorrow
            And leaden-eyed despairs,
    Where Beauty cannot keep her lustrous eyes,
        Or new Love pine at them beyond to-morrow.

4

Away ! away ! for I will fly to thee,
    Not charioted by Bacchus and his pards,
But on the viewless wings of Poesy,
    Though the dull brain perplexes and retards :
Already with thee ! tender is the night,
    And haply the Queen-Moon is on her throne,
        Cluster'd around by all her starry Fays ;

杯沿明滅著珍珠的泡沫，
　　給嘴唇染上紫斑；
哦，我要一飲而悄然離開塵寰，
　　和你同去幽暗的林中隱沒：

3

遠遠地、遠遠隱沒，讓我忘掉
　　你在樹葉間從不知道的一切，
忘記這疲勞、熱病、和焦躁，
　　這使人對坐而悲嘆的世界；
在這裏，青春蒼白、削瘦、死亡，
　　而「癱瘓」有幾根白髮在搖擺；
　　　在這裏，稍一思索就充滿了
　　　　憂傷和灰眼的絕望，
　　而「美」保持不住明眸的光彩，
　　　新生的愛情活不到明天就枯凋。

4

去吧！去吧！我要朝你飛去，
　　不用和酒神坐文豹的車駕，
我要展開詩歌底無形羽翼，
　　儘管這頭腦已經困頓、疲乏；
去了！啊，我已經和你同往！
　　夜這般溫柔，月后正登上寶座，
　　　周圍是侍衛她的一群星星；

137

But here there is no light,

Save what from heaven is with the breezes blown

Through verdurous glooms and winding mossy ways.

5

I cannot see what flowers are at my feet,

Nor what soft incense hangs upon the boughs,

But, in embalmed darkness, guess each sweet

Wherewith the seasonable month endows

The grass, the thicket, and the fruit-tree wild ;

White hawthorn, and the pastoral eglantine ;

Fast fading violets cover'd up in leaves ;

And mid-May's eldest child,

The coming musk-rose, full of dewy wine,

The murmurous haunt of flies on summer eves.

6

Darkling I listen ; and, for many a time

I have been half in love with easeful Death,

Call'd him soft names in many a mused rhyme,

To take into the air my quiet breath ;

Now more than ever seems it rich to die,

To cease upon the midnight with no pain,

While thou art pouring forth thy soul abroad

In such an ecstasy !

但這兒卻不甚明亮，
　　除了有一線天光，被微風帶過
　　　蔥綠的幽暗，和苔蘚的曲徑。

5

我看不出是哪種花草在腳旁，
　　什麼清香的花掛在樹枝上；
在溫馨的幽暗裏，我只能猜想
　　這個時令該把哪種芬芳
賦予這果樹，林莽，和草叢，
　　這白枳花，和田野的玫瑰，
　　　這綠葉堆中易謝的紫羅蘭，
　　　　　還有五月中旬的驕寵，
　　這綴滿了露酒的麝香薔薇，
　　　它成了夏夜蚊蚋的嗡嗡的港灣。

6

我在黑暗裏傾聽；啊，多少次
　　我幾乎愛上了靜謐的死亡，
我在詩思裏用盡了好的言辭，
　　求他把我的一息散入空茫；
　　而現在，哦，死更是多麼富麗：
在午夜裏溘然魂離人間，
　　當你正傾瀉著你的心懷
　　　發出這般的狂喜！

Still wouldst thou sing, and I have ears in vain —
    To thy high requiem become a sod.

7

Thou wast not born for death, immortal Bird !
    No hungry generations tread thee down ;
The voice I hear this passing night was heard
    In ancient days by emperor and clown :
Perhaps the self-same song that found a path
    Through the sad heart of Ruth, when, sick for home,
        She stood in tears amid the alien corn ;
            The same that oft-times hath
Charm'd magic casements, opening on the foam
    Of perilous seas, in faery lands forlorn.

8

Forlorn ! the very word is like a bell
    To toll me back from thee to my sole self !
Adieu ! the fancy cannot cheat so well
    As she is fam'd to do, deceiving elf.
Adieu ! adieu ! thy plaintive anthem fades

你仍將歌唱，但我卻不再聽見 ——

　　你的葬歌只能唱給泥草一塊。

7

永生的鳥啊，你不會死去！

　　飢餓的世代無法將你踐蹋；

今夜，我偶然聽到的歌曲

　　曾使古代的帝王和村夫喜悅

或許這同樣的歌也曾激蕩

　　露絲*憂鬱的心，使她不禁落淚，

　　　站在異邦的穀田裏想著家；

　　　　就是這聲音常常

在失掉了的仙域裏引動窗扉：

　　一個美女望著大海險惡的浪花。**

8

啊，失掉了！這句話好比一聲鐘

　　使我猛省到我站腳的地方！

別了！幻想，這騙人的妖童，

　　不能老耍弄它盛傳的伎倆。

別了！別了！你怨訴的歌聲

---

* 　據《舊約》，露絲是大衛王的祖先，原籍莫艾伯，以後在伯利恆爲富人波兹種田，並
　　且嫁給了他。

** 中世紀的傳奇故事往往描寫一個奇異的古堡，孤立在大海中；勇敢的騎士如果能冒險
　　來到這裏，定會得到財寶和古堡中的公主爲妻。這裏講到，夜鶯的歌會引動美人打開
　　窗戶，遙望並期待她的騎士來援救她脫離險境。

Past the near meadows, over the still stream,

    Up the hill-side ; and now 'tis buried deep

        In the next valley- glades :

Was it a vision, or a waking dream ?

    Fled is that music : — Do I wake or sleep ?

流過草坪，越過幽靜的溪水，

　　溜上山坡；而此時，它正深深

　　　　埋在附近的谿谷中：

噫，這是個幻覺，還是夢寐？

　　那歌聲去了： —— 我是睡？是醒？

1819年5月

Ode on a Grecian Urn

1

THOU still unravish'd bride of quietness,
    Thou foster-child of silence and slow time,
Sylvan historian, who canst thus express
    A flowery tale more sweetly than our rhyme :
What leaf-fring'd legend haunts about thy shape
      Of deities or mortals, or of both,
          in Tempe or the dales of Arcady ?
      What men or gods are these ?   What maidens loth?
What mad pursuit ?   What struggle to escape ?
        What pipes and timbrels ?   What wild ecstasy ?

2

Heard melodies are sweet, but those unheard
    Are sweeter ; therefore, ye soft pipes, play on ;
Not to the sensual ear, but, more endear'd,
    Pipe to the spirit ditties of no tone :
Fair youth, beneath the trees, thou canst not leave
    Thy song, nor ever can those trees be bare ;

希臘古甕頌

1

你委身「寂靜」的、完美的處子，
　　受過了「沉默」和「悠久」的撫育，
啊，田園的史家，你竟能鋪叙
　　一個如花的故事，比詩還瑰麗：
在你的形體上，豈非繚繞著
　　古老的傳說，以綠葉爲其邊緣，
　　　講著人，或神，敦陂或阿卡狄？*
　啊，是怎樣的人，或神！　在舞樂前
多熱烈的追求！　少女怎樣地逃躲！
　　　怎樣的風笛和鼓鐃！　怎樣的狂喜！

2

聽見的樂聲雖好，但若聽不見
　　卻更美；所以，吹吧，柔情的風笛；
不是奏給耳朵聽，而是更甜，
　　它給靈魂奏出無聲的樂曲；
樹下的美少年啊，你無法中斷
　　你的歌，那樹木也落不了葉子；

---

* 敦陂（Tempe），古希臘西沙裏的山谷，以風景優美著稱。阿卡狄（Arcady）山谷也是牧
　歌中常歌頌的樂園。

Bold Lover, never, never canst thou kiss,

Though winning near the goal — yet, do not grieve ;

    She cannot fade, though thou hast not thy bliss,

    For ever wilt thou love, and she be fair !

3

Ah, happy, happy boughs ! that cannot shed

    Your leaves, nor ever bid the Spring adieu ;

And, happy melodist, unwearied,

    For ever piping songs for ever new ;

More happy love ! more happy, happy love !

    For ever warm and still to be enjoy'd,

        For ever panting, and for ever young ;

All breathing human passion far above,

    That leaves a heart high-sorrowful and cloy'd,

        A burning forehead, and a parching tongue.

4

Who are these coming to the sacrifice ?

    To what green altar, O mysterious priest,

Lead'st thou that heifer lowing at the skies,

    And all her silken flanks with garlands drest ?

What little town by river or sea shore,

    Or mountain-built with peaceful citadel,

        Is emptied of this folk, this pious morn ?

鹵莽的戀人，你永遠、永遠吻不上，
雖然夠接近了 —— 但不必心酸；
　她不會老，雖然你不能如願以償，
　　你將永遠愛下去，她也永遠秀麗！

3

啊，幸福的樹木！你的枝葉
　不會剝落，從不曾離開春天；
幸福的吹笛人也不會停歇，
　他的歌曲永遠是那麼新鮮；
啊，更為幸福的、幸福的愛！
　永遠熱烈，正等待情人宴饗，
　　永遠熱情地心跳，永遠年輕；
幸福的是這一切超凡的情態：
　它不會使心靈饜足和悲傷，
　　沒有熾熱的頭腦，焦渴的嘴唇。

4

這些人是誰啊，都去赴祭祀？
　這作犧牲的小牛，對天鳴叫，
你要牽它到哪兒，神秘的祭司？
　花環綴滿著它光滑的身腰。
是從哪個傍河傍海的小鎮，
　或哪個靜靜的堡寨的山村，
　　來了這些人，在這敬神的清早？

147

And, little town, thy streets for evermore
　　Will silent be; and not a soul to tell
　　　Why thou art desolate, can e'er return.

　　　　5

O Attic shape !　Fair attitude !　with brede
　　Of marble men and maidens overwrought,
With forest branches and the trodden weed ;
　　Thou, silent form, dost tease us out of thought
As doth eternity :　Cold Pastoral !
　　When old age shall this generation waste,
　　　Thou shalt remain, in midst of other woe
Than ours, a friend to man, to whom thou say'st,
　　"Beauty is truth, truth beauty, "　— that is all
　　　Ye know on earth, and all ye need to know.

啊，小鎮，你的街道永遠恬靜；
　再也不可能回來一個靈魂
　　告訴人你何以是這麼寂寥。

5

哦，希臘的形狀！　唯美的觀照！
　上面綴有石雕的男人和女人，
還有林木，和踐踏過的青草；
　沉默的形體啊，你像是「永恆」
使人超越思想：啊，冰冷的牧歌！
　等暮年使這一世代都凋落，
　　只有你如舊；在另外的一些
憂傷中，你會撫慰後人說：
　「美即是眞，眞即是美，」這就包括
　　你們所知道、和該知道的一切。

1819年5月

Fancy

E VER let the Fancy roam,
    Pleasure never is at home :
At a touch sweet Pleasure melteth,
Like to bubbles when rain pelteth ;
Then let winged Fancy wander
Through the thought still spread beyond her :
Open wide the mind's cage- door,
She'll dart forth, and cloudward soar.
O sweet Fancy ! let her loose ;
Summer's joys are spoilt by use,   10
And the enjoying of the Spring
Fades as does its blossoming ;
Autumn's red-lipp'd fruitage too,
Blushing through the mist and dew,
Cloys with tasting : What do then ?
Sit thee by the ingle, when
The sear faggot blazes bright,
Spirit of a winter's night ;
When the soundless earth is muffled,
And the caked snow is shuffled   20
From the ploughboy's heavy shoon ;
When the Night doth meet the Noon

幻想

哦，讓幻想永遠漫遊，
快樂可不能被拘留：
只要一碰，甜蜜的快樂
就像水泡被雨點打破；
那麼，快讓有翅的幻想
隨著思想的推展遊蕩：
打開腦之門吧，這隻鳥
會衝出，飛到雲端繚繞。
哦，甜蜜的幻想！放開她，
夏季之樂已日久無華；
春天又能夠享受多久？
它已經隨著落花流走；
秋天的果實固然迷人，
從霧裏透出露水紅唇，
但嘗嘗就夠：那怎麼辦？
還是請你坐在爐邊，
看著乾柴熊熊地燃燒，
像冬夜的精靈在歡跳，
而死寂無聲的田野
覆蓋著一層平整的雪，
正被農夫的厚靴踢亂；
這時候，當子夜、白天

In a dark conspiracy

To banish Even from her sky.

Sit thee there, and send abroad,

With a mind self-overaw'd,

Fancy, high-commission'd : — send her !

She has vassals to attend her :

She will bring, in spite of frost,

Beauties that the earth hath lost ;   30

She will bring thee, all together,

All delights of summer weather ;

All the buds and bells of May,

From dewy sward or thorny spray ;

All the heaped Autumn's wealth,

With a still, mysterious stealth :

She will mix these pleasures up

Like three fit wines in a cup,

And thou shalt quaff it : — thou shalt hear   40

Distant harvest-carols clear ;

Rustle of the reaped corn ;

Sweet birds antheming the morn :

And, in the same moment — hark !

'Tis the early April lark,

Or the rooks, with busy caw,

Foraging for sticks and straw.

Thou shalt, at one glance, behold

正秘密地聚在一起
陰謀把黃昏逐出天宇，
你儘可坐下，讓心田
一片蕭穆，遠遠地派遣
幻想，給她一個使命，
她自有屬下替她執行；
儘管嚴寒，她會給帶來
大地已喪失的華彩。
啊，她會全部帶給你
又是夏令的各種樂趣，
又是五月的蓓蕾，蛊花，
從荊棘或草上摘下；
還有秋日的一切財富，
像是一種神秘的臟物；
她將把所有的樂趣
像三味好酒合在一起
飲乾它吧： —— 你會聽到
隱隱的收割者的歌謠，
穀穗的沙沙的聲音，
還有小鳥在歌唱清晨；
而同時，聽！那是雲雀
鳴囀在早春的四月，
或是烏鴉不停地咭噪，
忙於尋索樹枝和稻草。
只消一眼，你就會看見

The daisy and the marigold ;
White-plum'd lilies, and the first
Hedge-grown primrose that hath burst ;   50
Shaded hyacinth, alway
Sapphire queen of the mid-May ;
And every leaf, and every flower
Pearled with the self-same shower.
Thou shalt see the field-mouse peep
Meagre from its celled sleep ;
And the snake all winter-thin
Cast on sunny bank its skin ;
Freckled nest-eggs thou shalt see
Hatching in the hawthorn-tree,   60
When the hen-bird's wing doth rest
Quiet on her mossy nest ;
Then the hurry and alarm
When the bee-hive casts its swarm ;
Acorns ripe down-pattering,
While the autumn breezes sing.

       Oh, sweet Fancy ! let her loose ;
Every thing is spoilt by use :
Where's the cheek that doth not fade,
Too much gaz'd at ?   Where's the maid   70
Whose lip mature is ever new ?

雛菊，金盞花，和籬邊
初開的櫻草，點點黃色，
還有白綾的野百合，
還有紫菫，五月中旬的
花后，在樹蔭裏隱蔽；
那每一片葉，每一朵花
都在同一陣雨露下
掛上珍珠。 你還會看見
田鼠在窺視，不再冬眠；
蟄居的瘦蛇見了陽光，
把它的皮脫在河岸上；
你會看見在山櫨樹上，
靜靜地，雌鳥的翅膀
正覆在生苔的巢裏，
把有斑點的卵孵育；
而後飛來了一群蜜蜂
就引起騷亂和驚恐；
成熟的橡實打在地上，
秋風正在輕輕地歌唱。

　　哦，甜蜜的幻想！放開她，
萬物都日久而失華：
哪裏有不褪色的人面？
哪一個少女百看不厭？
她的紅唇會永遠新鮮？

Where's the eye, however blue,
Doth not weary?   Where's the face
One would meet in every place ?
Where's the voice, however soft,
One would hear so very oft ?
At a touch sweet Pleasure melteth
Like to bubbles when rain pelteth.
Let, then, winged Fancy find
Thee a mistress to thy mind :   80
Dulcet-eyed as Ceres' daughter,
Ere the God of Torment taught her
How to frown and how to chide ;
With a waist and with a side
White as Hebe's, when her zone
Slipt its golden clasp, and down
Fell her kirtle to her feet,
While she held the goblet sweet,
And Jove grew languid. — Break the mesh
Of the Fancy's silken leash ;   90
Quickly break her prison-string
And such joys as these she' ll bring. —
Let the winged Fancy roam,
Pleasure never is at home.

她那眼睛，無論多藍，
怎能夠長久保持魅力？
哪兒有一種柔聲細語，
能夠聽來永遠不變？
哪個人能夠永遠看見？
只要一碰，甜蜜的快樂
就像水泡被雨點打破。
那麼，快讓有翅的幻想
給你找個中意的姑娘，
讓她有美妙的眼睛
嫵媚得像普洛斯嬪，＊
因為痛苦之神還未教她
怎樣皺眉，怎樣責罰；
要讓她的腰身潔白
有如希比，＊＊讓她的腰帶
脫落金鉤，上衣落到腳前，
手裏拿著青春的金盞 ——
而約甫醉了。　啊，快解開
糾纏著幻想的絲帶；
只要打碎了她的牢獄，
她就會帶來各種樂趣。
哦，讓幻想永遠漫遊，
快樂可不能被拘留。

1818年8－12月

＊　據希臘神話，普洛斯嬪是一個美女，被地獄之神普魯東盜去，成為冥后。
＊＊　希比是天神宙斯（約甫）和赫拉之女，主宰青春的女神。她經常在諸神之前侍酒。

Ode

BARDS of Passion and of Mirth,
    Ye have left your souls on earth !
Have ye souls in heaven too,
Double-lived in regions new ?
Yes, and those of heaven commune
With the spheres of sun and moon ;
With the noise of fountains wond'rous,
And the parle of voices thund'rous ;
With the whisper of heaven's trees
And one another, in soft ease   10
Seated on Elysian lawns
Brows'd by none but Dian's fawns ;
Underneath large blue-bells tented,
Where the daisies are rose-scented,
And the rose herself has got
Perfume which on earth is not ;
Where the nightingale doth sing
Not a senseless, tranced thing,
But divine melodious truth ;
Philosophic numbers smooth ;   20

頌詩*

歌唱「情欲」和「歡樂」的詩人
人間留下了你們的靈魂！
你們是否也逍遙天上，
同時生存在兩個地方？
是的，你們的在天之靈
成了太陽和月亮的知心，
伴著神異的噴泉喧響，
和雷的鳴聲一起振蕩；
你們和天庭的樹葉低語，
你們彼此會談，恬靜地
坐在極樂園的草地上，
以蔚藍的花朵作屏障；
在那兒，月神的鹿在吃草，
雛菊發出玫瑰的味道，
而玫瑰另有一種香氣
是人間未曾有過的馥郁；
夜鶯在那兒所唱的歌
不是毫無意義的歡樂，
而是悅耳的至高的真理，
是智慧的悠揚的歌曲，

---

* 本詩是寫在英國十七世紀劇作家波芒和弗萊齊（Beaumont and Fletcher）的悲喜劇《旅店中的美女》的空白上面的。

159

Tales and golden histories
Of heaven and its mysteries.

Thus ye live on high, and then
On the earth ye live again ;
And the souls ye left behind you
Teach us, here, the way to find you,
Where your other souls are joying,
Never slumber'd, never cloying.
Here, your earth-born souls still speak
To mortals, of their little week ;   30
Of their sorrows and delights ;
Of their passions and their spites ;
Of their glory and their shame ;
What doth strengthen and what maim.
Thus ye teach us, every day,
Wisdom, though fled far away.

Bards of Passion and of Mirth,
Ye have left your souls on earth !
Ye have souls in heaven too,
Double-lived in regions new !   40

是金色的歷史和掌故
把天庭的秘密一一吐露。

　啊，就這樣，你們住在天空，
但在地面你們也生存；
你們的遺魂告訴了世人
怎樣前去把你們訪尋，
尋到靈魂的另一個居處，
看你們歡樂，從不饜足。
在這兒，你們塵世的靈魂
還在敘述自己的一生，
講著那短短的一個星期：
愛和恨，憂傷和歡喜，
講著自己的恥辱和光榮，
什麼慰藉，什麼在刺痛。
就這樣，你們每天都敎人
智慧，雖然早已飄逝無蹤。

　歌唱「情慾」和「歡樂」的詩人，
人間留下了你們的靈魂！
你們是否也逍遙天上，
同時生存在兩個地方？

1818年8－12月

Lines on the Mermaid Tavern

SOULS of Poets dead and gone,
    What Elysium have ye known,
Happy field or mossy cavern,
Choicer than the Mermaid Tavern ?
Have ye tippled drink more fine
Than mine host's Canary wine ?
Or are fruits of Paradise
Sweeter than those dainty pies
Of venison ?   O generous food !
Drest as though bold Robin Hood   10
Would, with his maid Marian,
Sup and bowse from horn and can.

    I have heard that on a day
Mine host's sign-board flew away,
Nobody knew whither, till
An astrologer's old quill
To a sheepskin gave the story,
Said he saw you in your glory,
Underneath a new old-sign

詠「美人魚」酒店*

啊，亡故的詩人的幽靈，
你們看過哪個青苔洞，
哪個極樂世界或桃源，
比得上「美人魚」酒店？
你們飲過哪種仙品
比它那葡萄酒更芳醇？
是否天堂裏的花果
有一種美味能勝過
它的鹿肉餅？　啊，美味！
好像羅賓漢就會
用角杯盛上這種飲料，
和他的姑娘痛飲通宵。

　我聽說，有一天，老闆，
他的招牌被颳上天，
沒有人知道飛往哪裏，
直到星象家的鵝毛筆
在羊皮紙上講了出來，
據說，他看見你很光彩，
正坐在另一家老字號

* 「美人魚」酒店是倫敦最早的一家文人薈萃的酒店，莎士比亞、約翰‧敦（John Donne, 1571—1631）、波芒和弗萊齊常到那裏去。

Sipping beverage divine,   20

And pledging with contented smack

The Mermaid in the Zodiac.

    Souls of Poets dead and gone,

What Elysium have ye known,

Happy field or mossy cavern,

Choicer than the Mermaid Tavern ?

啜飲著神仙的飲料，
並且保證要把「美人魚」
開設在黃道十二宮裏。

　啊，亡故的詩人的幽靈，
你們看過哪個青苔洞，
哪個極樂世界或桃源，
比得上「美人魚」酒店？

1818年

Robin Hood

To a Friend

NO! those days are gone away,
　　　And their hours are old and gray,
And their minutes buried all
Under the down-trodden pall
Of the leaves of many years :
Many times have winter's shears,
Frozen North, and chilling East,
Sounded tempests to the feast
Of the forest's whispering fleeces,
Since men knew nor rent nor leases.　　　　10

　　No, the bugle sounds no more,
And the twanging bow no more ;
Silent is the ivory shrill
Past the heath and up the hill ;
There is no mid-forest laugh,
Where lone Echo gives the half
To some wight, amaz'd to hear
Jesting, deep in forest drear.

羅賓漢*

致一友人

是的！那個時代消逝了，
它的時刻已經蒼老，
它的每一分鐘都埋在
多年的落葉下，任未來
把它踐踏一遍又一遍；
多少次了，冬季的刀剪，
冷峭的東風，北國的嚴寒，
帶給林中落葉的華筵
一陣騷動，啊，早自人類
還不知道有所謂租稅。

是的，喇叭已經不響了，
錚鳴的弓也沒有了，
角笛的尖聲已經沉寂，
越過荒原，沒入群山裏；
林中再也聽不見大笑 ——
一脈回音斷續地飄，
使哪個村夫感到詫異：
荒林深處有誰在打趣！

---

* 羅賓漢是英國民間傳說的俠盜，約生於十三世紀，有不少民歌及故事記述他及他的同
　夥。他體現了過去人民愛自由及反抗不合理社會的理想。

On the fairest time of June
You may go, with sun or moon,
Or the seven stars to light you,
Or the polar ray to right you ;
But you never may behold
Little John, or Robin bold ;
Never one, of all the clan,
Thrumming on an empty can
Some old hunting ditty, while
He doth his green way beguile
To fair hostess Merriment,
Down beside the pasture Trent ;
For he left the merry tale
Messenger for spicy ale.

    Gone, the merry morris din ;
Gone, the song of Gamelyn ;
Gone, the tough-belted outlaw
Idling in the "grenè shawe ;"
All are gone away and past !
And if Robin should be cast
Sudden from his turfed grave,

在六月的美好的時光
你可以趁著太陽、月亮、
或七顆星座的光明，
或藉著北極光的指引，
儘你去走，你不會遇見
勇敢的羅賓，或小約翰；
你不會遇到任何好漢
用手彈著一只空鐵罐，
沿著綠徑自在逍遙，
口哼一支獵人的小調，
去找他的女主人「歡樂」，
在純特草原邊上經過；
因為啊，他已經遺留
一個快樂的故事下酒。

　　完了，化裝舞會的歡騰，
完了，甘米林＊的歌聲，
完了，那無畏的強盜
不再在綠林裏逍遙；
一切去了，一切都不見！
即使羅賓漢啊，突然
跳出他青草的墳頭，

＊ 甘米林是喬叟《甘米林的故事》中的綠林英雄。

169

And if Marian should have 40
Once again her forest days,
She would weep, and he would craze :
He would swear, for all his oaks,
Fall'n beneath the dockyard strokes,
Have rotted on the briny seas ;
She would weep that her wild bees
Sang not to her — strange ! that honey
Can't be got without hard money !

So it is : yet let us sing ,
Honour to the old bow-string ! 50
Honour to the bugle-horn !
Honour to the woods unshorn !
Honour to the Lincoln green !
Honour to the archer keen !
Honour to tight little John,
And the horse he rode upon !
Honour to bold Robin Hood,
Sleeping in the underwood !
Honour to maid Marian,
And to all the Sherwood-clan ! 60
Though their days have hurried by
Let us two a burden try.

即使瑪麗安又能夠
在樹林裏消磨時光，
她會哭的，而他會發狂，
因為他所有的橡樹
都已成為造船的大木
在鹹澀的海上腐爛，
她會哭泣，因為再也不見
蜜蜂對她歌唱 ── 多驚奇！
沒有錢就得不到蜂蜜！

　　好吧：但讓我們唱一遍，
紀念那古老的弓弦！
向角笛和綠色的森林，
向林肯鎮的布衫致敬！
唱一唱弓手的神箭，
還有短小精悍的約翰
和他那馬兒。且讓我們
向勇敢的羅賓漢致敬，
他正在灌木叢裏安眠！
還有他的姑娘瑪麗安
和舍伍得的一夥好漢！
儘管他們的日子不再，
讓我們唱支歌兒開懷。

1818年2月

To Autumn

1

SEASON of mists and mellow fruitfulness,
    Close bosom-friend of the maturing sun ;
Conspiring with him how to load and bless
    With fruit the vines that round the thatch-eves run ;
To bend with apples the moss'd cottage-trees,
    And fill all fruit with ripeness to the core ;
        To swell the gourd, and plump the hazel shells
    With a sweet kernel ; to set budding more,
And still more, later flowers for the bees,
Until they think warm days will never cease,
        For Summer has o'er-brimm'd their clammy cells.

2

Who hath not seen thee oft amid thy store ?
    Sometimes whoever seeks abroad may find
Thee sitting careless on a granary floor,
    Thy hair soft-lifted by the winnowing wind ;
Or on a half- reap'd furrow sound asleep,

秋頌*

1

霧氣洋溢、果實圓熟的秋，
　　你和成熟的太陽成爲友伴；
你們密謀用纍纍的珠球
　　綴滿茅屋檐下的葡萄藤蔓；
使屋前的老樹背負著蘋果，
　　讓熟味透進果實的心中，
　　　使葫蘆脹大，鼓起了榛子殼，
　　好塞進甜核；又爲了蜜蜂
一次一次開放過遲的花朶，
使它們以爲日子將永遠暖和，
　　　因爲夏季早塡滿它們的黏巢。

2

誰不經常看見你伴著穀倉
　　在田野裏也可以把你找到，
你有時隨意坐在打麥場上，
　　讓髮絲隨著簸穀的風輕飄；
有時候，爲罌粟花香所沉迷，

＊ 本詩有些詞句，參照了朱湘《番石榴集》的譯文。

Drows'd with the fume of poppies, while thy hook

  Spares the next swath and all its twined flowers :

And sometimes like a gleaner thou dost keep

  Steady thy laden head across a brook ;

  Or by a cyder-press, with patient look,

   Thou watchest the last oozings hours by hours.

   3

Where are the songs of Spring ? Ay, where are they ?

  Think not of them, thou hast thy music too, —

While barred clouds bloom the soft-dying day,

  And touch the stubble-plains with rosy hue ;

Then in a wailful choir the small gnats mourn

  Among the river sallows, borne aloft

   Or sinking as the light wind lives or dies ;

And full-grown lambs loud bleat from hilly bourn ;

  Hedge-crickets sing ; and now with treble soft

  The red-breast whistles from a garden-croft ;

   And gathering swallows twitter in the skies.

你倒臥在收割一半的田壟，

　　讓鐮刀歇在下一畦的花旁；

或者，像拾穗人越過小溪，

　　你昂首背著穀袋，投下倒影，

　　或者就在榨果架下坐幾點鐘，

　　　你耐心瞧著徐徐滴下的酒漿。

3

啊，春日的歌哪裏去了？　但不要

　　想這些吧，你也有你的音樂 ——

當波狀的雲把將逝的一天映照，

　　以胭紅抹上殘梗散碎的田野，

這時啊，河柳下的一群小飛蟲

　　就同奏哀音，它們忽而飛高，

　　　忽而下落，隨著微風的起滅；

籬下的蟋蟀在歌唱；在園中

　　紅胸的知更鳥就群起呼哨；

　　而群羊在山圈裏高聲咩叫；

　　　叢飛的燕子在天空呢喃不歇。

1819年9月19日

175

Ode on Melancholy

1

NO, no, go not to Lethe, neither twist
    Wolf's-bane, tight-rooted, for its poisonous wine ;
Nor suffer thy pale forehead to be kiss'd
    By nightshade, ruby grape of Proserpine ;
Make not your rosary of yew-berries,
    Nor let the beetle, nor the death-moth be
      Your mournful Psyche, nor the downy owl
A partner in your sorrow's mysteries ;
    For shade to shade will come too drowsily,
      And drown the wakeful anguish of the soul.

2

But when the melancholy fit shall fall
    Sudden from heaven like a weeping cloud,
That fosters the droop-headed flowers all,
    And hides the green hill in an April shroud ;
Then glut thy sorrow on a morning rose,
    Or on the rainbow of the salt sand-wave,

憂鬱頌

1

不，不要去到忘川吧，不要
　　擰出附子草的毒汁當酒飲，
無須讓普洛斯嬪的紅葡萄 ——
　　龍葵，和你蒼白的額角親吻；
別用水松果殼當你的念珠，
　　也別讓甲蟲或者飛蛾充作
　　　哀憐你的賽姬*吧，更別讓夜梟
作伴，把隱秘的悲哀訴給它聽；
　　因爲陰影不宜於找陰影結合，
　　　那會使心痛得昏沉，不再清醒。

2

當憂鬱的情緒突然襲來，
　　像是啜泣的陰雲，降自天空，
像是陣雨使小花昂起頭來，
　　把青山遮在四月的白霧中，
你啊，該讓你的悲哀滋養於
　　早晨的玫瑰，錦簇團團的牡丹，

---

* 賽姬，據希臘神話，是國王的女兒，爲愛神邱比特所戀，但因以燈盞的熱油燙傷了愛神，他一怒而去。賽姬悲哀地到處尋找他，經過許多困苦，最後如願以償。

Or on the wealth of globed peonies ;
Or if thy mistress some rich anger shows,
   Emprison her soft hand, and let her rave,
      And feed deep, deep upon her peerless eyes.

3

She dwells with Beauty — Beauty that must die ;
   And Joy, whose hand is ever at his lips
Bidding adieu ; and aching Pleasure nigh,
   Turning to poison while the bee-mouth sips :
Ay, in the very temple of Delight
   Veil'd Melancholy has her sovran shrine,
      Though seen of none save him whose strenuous tongue
   Can burst Joy's grape against his palate fine ;
His soul shall taste the sadness of her might,
      And be among her cloudy trophies hung.

或者是海波上的一道彩虹；

或者，如若你的戀女*生了氣，

　拉住她的柔手吧，讓她去胡言，

　　深深地啜飲她那美妙的眼睛。

3

和她同住的有「美」—— 生而必死；

　還有「喜悅」，永遠在吻「美」的嘴唇

和他告別；還有「歡笑」是鄰居

　啊，痛人的「歡笑」，只要蜜蜂來飲，

它就變成毒汁。隱蔽的「憂鬱」

　原在「快樂」底殿堂中設有神壇，

　　雖然，只有以健全而知味的口

　咀嚼「喜悅」之酸果的人才能看見；

他的心靈一旦碰到她的威力，

　　會立即被俘獲，懸掛在雲頭。

1819年5月

---

* 指「憂鬱」

Hymn to Apollo

1

GOD of the golden bow,
    And of the golden lyre,
And of the golden hair,
    And of the golden fire,
      Charioteer
      Of the patient year,
    Where — where slept thine ire,
When like a blank idiot I put on thy wreath,
    Thy laurel, thy glory,
    The light of thy story,
Or was I a worm — too low crawling, for death ?
    O Delphic Apollo !

2

    The Thunderer grasp'd and grasp'd,
      The Thunderer frown'd and frown'd ;
    The eagle's feathery mane
      For wrath became stiffen'd — the sound

阿波羅禮讚

1

大神啊，你有金琴，
　　還有金色的頭髮；
你有金色的火焰，
　　還有金弓一把；
　　　　駕著車環行
　　　　四季遲緩的旅程；
　　請問你的怒火在哪裏伏下？
難道你能容忍我冠戴你的榮譽，
　　你的花冠，你的桂花，
　　你的故事的光華？
或者我是蛆蟲 —— 不值死的一擊？
　　哦，狄爾菲的阿波羅！

2

掌雷的天神*握拳又握拳，
　　掌雷的天神皺眉又縐眉；
巨鷹的鬃髮般的羽毛
　　憤怒得根根豎立 —— 而劈雷

---

* 指雷神宙斯，他有巨鷹在身側。

181

Of breeding thunder

Went drowsily under,

Muttering to be unbound.

O why didst thou pity, and for a worm

Why touch thy soft lute

Till the thunder was mute,

Why was not I crush'd — such a pitiful germ?

O Delphic Apollo !

3

The Pleiades were up,

Watching the silent air ;

The seeds and roots in the Earth

Were swelling for summer fare ;

The Ocean, its neighbour,

Was at its old labour,

When, who — who did dare

To tie, like a madman, thy plant round his brow,

And grin and look proudly,

And blaspheme so loudly,

And live for that honour, to stoop to thee now ?

O Delphic Apollo !

才蘊育它的聲音，

卻又逐漸消沉，

喃喃著，不得脫手而飛。

哦，為什麼你不忍，要為蛆蟲求情？

為什麼你要輕彈金琴

使巨雷啞然無音，

為什麼不讓它摧毀這可鄙的微菌？

哦，狄爾菲的阿波羅！

3

七姊妹的星辰起來了，

她們守著空中的靜寂；

埋在地下的種子和根芽

正在鼓脹，等著宴饗夏季：

大地的鄰居，海波，

也做著古老的工作，

啊，這一刻，有誰、誰敢於

發瘋似地，在額前扎上你的花草，

驕傲地冷笑和四顧，

如此高聲地把神褻瀆，

而還以此為榮，因為現在就向你伏倒？*

哦，狄爾菲的阿波羅！

1816年

* 這裏的意思似乎是，詩人自謙他過早以其詩歌炫耀於世，其實這還不是詩歌出現的時
代，因此他之對阿波羅「伏倒」，正是褻瀆了阿波羅。

What the Thrush said

To Reynolds

O THOU whose face hath felt the Winter's wind,
    Whose eye has seen the snow-clouds hung in mist
And the black elm tops 'mong the freezing stars !
To thee the spring will be a harvest time.
O thou whose only book has been the light
Of supreme darkness, which thou feddest on
Night after night, when Phœbus was away !
To thee the Spring shall be a triple morn.
O fret not after knowledge.   I have none,
And yet my song comes native with the warmth.
O fret not after knowledge !   I have none,
And yet the evening listens.   He who saddens
At thought of idleness cannot be idle,
And he's awake who thinks himself asleep.

畫眉鳥的話*

給瑞諾茲**

啊，你的臉上撲過多天的風，
你曾看見雪絮的雲霧瀰漫，
黑色的榆枝插上冰冷的星天！
等著吧，春天將是你豐收的季節。
啊，極度的黑暗曾是你唯一的
學識的明光，在日神離開後，
一夜又一夜，你以它為營養！
等著吧，春天定是燦爛的黎明。
別急於求知吧。　我一點沒有；
但我的歌卻和溫暖的天同調。
別急於求知吧！　我一點沒有；
但黃昏卻在聆聽。　凡是憂心於
無事可做的人，是不懶散的；
那自以為睡的，他必定清醒。

1818年2月

＊　批評家曾指出，本詩以半似重複的語句，傳出了畫眉歌唱的節奏。原詩無韻。
＊＊　瑞諾茲（John H. Reynolds, 1796—1852），英國詩人，濟慈的好友。

Faery Songs

SHED no tear ! oh shed no tear !
  The flower will bloom another year.
Weep no more ! oh weep no more !
Young buds sleep in the root's white core.
Dry your eyes ! oh dry your eyes !
For I was taught in Paradise
To ease my breast of melodies —
    Shed no tear.

Overhead ! look overhead !
'Mong the blossoms white and red —   10
Look up, look up. I flutter now
On this flush pomegranate bough.
See me ! 'tis this silvery bill
Ever cures the good man's ill.
Shed no tear ! Oh shed no tear !
The flower will bloom another year.
Adieu, adieu ! — I fly, adieu !
I vanish in the heaven's blue —
    Adieu ! Adieu !

仙靈之歌

不要悲哀吧！哦，不要悲哀！
到明年，花兒還會盛開。
不要落淚吧！哦，不要落淚！
花苞正在根的深心裏睡。
擦乾眼睛吧！擦乾你的眼睛！
因爲我曾在樂園裏學會
怎樣傾瀉出內心的樂音 ——
　　　　　　哦，不要落淚。

往頭上看啊！往頭上看！
在那紅白的花簇中間 ——
抬頭看，抬頭看。　我正歡跳
在這豐滿的石榴枝條。
看哪！就是用這銀白的嘴
我永遠醫治善心的傷悲。
不要悲哀吧！　哦，不要悲哀！
到明年，花兒還會盛開。
別了，別了！ —— 我飛了，再見！
我要沒入天空的蔚藍 ——
　　　　　　哦，再見，再見！

1818年

Daisy's Song

1

THE sun, with his great eye,
   Sees not so much as I ;
And the moon, all silver-proud,
Might as well be in a cloud.

2

And O the spring — the spring !
I lead the life of a king !
Couch'd in the teeming grass,
I spy each pretty lass.

3

I look where no one dares,
And I stare where no one stares,
And when the night is nigh,
Lambs bleat my lullaby.

雛菊之歌

1

太陽，雖然它眼睛大睜，
遠不如我看得多而清；
那驕傲的銀色的月亮，
雲彩遮不遮，反正一樣。

2

哦，來了春天，春天多好，
我就像帝王一樣逍遙！
我躺在茂盛的青草上，
偷看每個漂亮的姑娘。

3

我窺進人所不到之處，
看那人不敢看的事物；
而如果黑夜悄悄來了，
羊群就咩咩催我睡覺。

1818年

Where be ye going, you Devon Maid ?

1

WHERE be ye going, you Devon maid ?
  And what have ye there in the basket ?
Ye tight little fairy, just fresh from the dairy,
  Will ye give me some cream if I ask it ?

2

I love your Meads, and I love your flowers,
  And I love your junkets mainly,
But 'hind the door I love kissing more,
  O look not so disdainly.

3

I love your hills and I love your dales,
  And I love your flocks a-bleating —
But O, on the heather to lie together,
  With both our hearts a-beating !

4

I'll put your basket all safe in a nook ;
  Your shawl I'll hang on the willow ;

狄萬的姑娘

你到哪兒去呀，狄萬的姑娘？
　你的提筐裏裝的是什麼？
你從牛奶房來的小仙女兒，
　行不行，要是我討一點乳酪？

2

我愛你的草坪，我愛你的花朵，
　我很愛你的乳酥食品；
如果在門後，我更愛偷偷吻你，
　唷，別這麼輕蔑地看人。

3

我愛你的山峰，我愛你的山谷，
　我還愛你的羊兒咩叫，
我多願意在灌木下和你躺著，
　聽我們的兩顆心歡跳！

4

那我就把你的提筐放在一隅，
　把你的披肩掛上楊柳，

And we will sigh in the daisy's eye,

And kiss on a grass green pillow.

我們將只對著雛菊輕嘆，接吻，
　用青青的草當作枕頭。

1818年3月

In a drear-nighted December

1

IN a drear-nighted December,
  Too happy, happy tree,
Thy branches ne' er remember
Their green felicity :
The north cannot undo them
With a sleety whistle through them ;
Nor frozen thawings glue them
From budding at the prime.

2

In a drear-nighted December,
Too happy, happy brook,   10
Thy bubblings ne' er remember
Apollo' s summer look ;
But with a sweet forgetting,
They stay their crystal fretting,
Never, never petting
About the frozen time.

「在寒夜的十二月裏」

1

在寒夜的十二月裏，
啊，快樂的、快樂的樹！
你的枝幹從不記得
自己的綠色的幸福：
北風夾著冰雹呼嘯，
卻摧不毀你的枝杈，
溶雪後的冷峭也不會
把你凍得綻不開花。

2

在寒夜的十二月裏，
啊，快樂的、快樂的小溪，
你的喋喋從不記得
阿波羅夏日的笑意；
你帶著甜蜜的遺忘
經歷過結晶的約束，
對於這冰凍的季節
從來、從來也不惱怒。

3

Ah ! would 'twere so with many
A gentle girl and boy !
But were there ever any
Writhed not at passed joy ?
To know the change and feel it,   20
When there is none to heal it
Nor numbed sense to steel it,
Was never said in rhyme.

3

唉！但願許多青年男女
也能夠和你們相同！
但對於逝去的歡樂
可有誰不心中絞痛？
儘管人感到了無常，
沒有辦法醫治這創傷，
而又不能自居爲草木，
這卻從不曾表於詩章。

1818年10－12月

La Belle Dame sans Merci

1

O WHAT can ail thee Knight at arms
  Alone and palely loitering ?
The sedge has withered from the Lake
  And no birds sing !

2

O what can ail thee Knight at arms
  So haggard, and so woe begone ?
The Squirrel's granary is full
  And the harvest's done.

3

I see a lilly on thy brow
  With anguish moist and fever dew,
And on thy cheeks a fading rose
  Fast withereth too —

4

I met a Lady in the Meads
  Full beautiful, a faery's child

無情的妖女

1

騎士啊，是什麼苦惱你，
　　獨自沮喪地遊蕩？
湖中的蘆葦已經枯了，
　　也沒有鳥兒歌唱！

2

騎士啊，是什麼苦惱你，
　　這般憔悴和悲傷？
松鼠的小巢貯滿食物，
　　莊稼也都進了穀倉。

3

你的額角白似百合
　　垂掛著熱病的露珠，
你的面頰像是玫瑰，
　　正在很快地凋枯。 ──

4

我在草坪上遇見了
　　一個妖女，美似天仙，

Her hair was long, her foot was light
    And her eyes were wild —

5

I made a Garland for her head,
    And bracelets too, and fragrant Zone
She look'd at me as she did love
    And made sweet moan —

6

I set her on my pacing steed
    And nothing else saw all day long
For sidelong would she bend and sing
    A faery's song —

7

She found me roots of relish sweet
    And honey wild and manna dew
And sure in language strange she said
    I love thee true —

8

She took me to her elfin grot
    And there she wept and sigh'd full sore,

她輕捷、長髮，而眼裏
　　野性的光芒閃閃。

5

我給她編織過花冠、
　　芬芳的腰帶和手鐲，
她柔聲地輕輕太息，
　　彷彿是真心愛我。

6

我帶她騎在駿馬上，
　　她把臉兒側對著我，
我整日什麼都不顧，
　　只聽她的妖女之歌。

7

她給採來美味的草根、
　　野蜜、甘露和仙果，
她用了一篇奇異的話，
　　說她是真心愛我。

8

她帶我到了她的山洞，
　　又是落淚，又是悲嘆，

And there I shut her wild wild eyes
     With kisses four.

9

And there she lulled me asleep
     And there I dream'd Ah Woe betide !
The latest dream I ever dreamt
     On the cold hill side

10

I saw pale Kings, and Princes too
     Pale warriors death pale were they all
They cried La belle dame sans merci
     Thee hath in thrall.

11

I saw their starv'd lips in the gloam
     With horrid warning gaped wide,
And I awoke, and found me here
     On the cold hill's side

12

And this is why I sojourn here
     Alone and palely loitering ;

我在那兒四次吻著
　　她野性的、野性的眼。

9

我被她迷得睡著了，
　　啊，做了個驚心的噩夢！
我看見國王和王子
　　也在那妖女的洞中，

10

還有無數的騎士，
　　都蒼白得像是骷髏；
他們叫道：無情的妖女
　　已把你作了俘囚！

11

在幽暗裏，他們的癟嘴
　　大張著，預告著災禍；
我一覺醒來，看見自己
　　躺在這冰冷的山坡。

12

因此，我就留在這兒，
　　獨自沮喪地遊蕩；

203

Though the sedge is withered from the Lake

And no birds sing — . . .

雖然湖中的蘆葦已枯，

也沒有鳥兒歌唱。

1819年4月28日

Isabella

or

the Pot of Basil

A Story from Boccaccio

1

F AIR Isabel, poor simple Isabel !
    Lorenzo, a young palmer in Love's eye !
They could not in the self-same mansion dwell
    Without some stir of heart, some malady ;
They could not sit at meals but feel how well
    It soothed each to be the other by ;
They could not, sure, beneath the same roof sleep
But to each other dream, and nightly weep.

2

With every morn their love grew tenderer,
    With every eve deeper and tenderer still ;
He might not in house, field, or garden stir,

伊莎貝拉*

（或「紫蘇花盆」）

── 取自薄伽丘的故事** ──

1

美麗的伊莎貝爾！真純的伊莎貝爾！

　　羅倫左，一個朝拜愛神的年輕人！

他們怎能並住在一所大廈裏

　　而不感到內心的騷擾和苦痛；

他們怎能坐下用餐而不感到

　　彼此靠近在一起是多麼稱心；

啊，是的！只要他們在同一屋檐下睡，

必然就夢見另一個人，夜夜落淚。

2

每一清早，他們的愛情增進一步，

　　每到黃昏，那愛情就更深刻而溫馨；

他無論在哪裏：室內、田野或園中，

---

*　原詩韻腳是12121233，譯詩改為在第一、三、五行上沒有韻。

**　薄伽丘（G. Boccaccio, 1313—1375），義大利作家，小說《十日談》即其名著。本篇情節取自《十日談》中第四日的第五篇故事，但與原來情節略有出入。原作為兄弟三人，濟慈改為二人，並以與貴族締親作為謀殺的動機。

But her full shape would all his seeing fill ;
And his continual voice was pleasanter
    To her, than noise of trees or hidden rill ;
Her lute-string gave an echo of his name,
She spoilt her half-done broidery with the same.

3

He knew whose gentle hand was at the latch
    Before the door had given her to his eyes ;
And from her Chamber-window he would catch
    Her beauty farther than the falcon spies ;
And constant as her vespers would he watch,
    Because her face was turn'd to the same skies ;
And with sick longing all the night outwear,
To hear her morning step upon the stair.

4

A whole long month of May in this sad plight
    Made their cheeks paler by the break of June :
"To-morrow will I bow to my delight,
    To-morrow will I ask my lady's boon. " —
"O may I never see another night,
    Lorenzo, if thy lips breathe not love's tune. " —
So spake they to their pillows ; but, alas,
Honeyless days and days did he let pass ;

他的眼簾必充滿她整個的身影；
而她呢，樹木和隱蔽溪水的喧嘩
　　無論怎樣清瀝，也不及他的聲音；
她的琵琶時時把他的名字迴蕩，
她的刺繡空下一半，也被那名字填上。

　　　　　　3

當房門還沒有透露她的身影，
　　他已經知道是誰的手握著門環；
朝她臥房的窗口，他窺視她的美，
　　那視力比鷹隼的還更銳利、深遠；
他總是在她作晚禱時仰望著她，
　　因為她的面孔也在仰對著青天；
一整夜他在病懨的相思中耗盡，
只為想聽她清早下樓的腳步聲音。

　　　　　　4

就這樣，整個漫長而憂鬱的五月
　　使戀人的臉蒼白了；等到六月初：
「明天，我一定要向我的喜悅俯首，
　　明天，我要向我的姑娘請求幸福。」──
「啊，羅倫左，我不願再活過一夜，
　　假如你的嘴唇還不把愛曲傾訴。」
這便是他們對枕頭的低語；唉，可是
他的日子還只是無精打采地消逝；

5

Until sweet Isabella's untouch'd cheek

 Fell sick within the rose's just domain,

Fell thin as a young mother's, who doth seek

 By every lull to cool her infant's pain :

"How ill she is," said he, "I may not speak,

 And yet I will, and tell my love all plain :

If looks speak love-laws, I will drink her tears,

And at the least 'twill startle off her cares."

6

So said he one fair morning, and all day

 His heart beat awfully against his side ;

And to his heart he inwardly did pray

 For power to speak ; but still the ruddy tide

Stifled his voice, and puls'd resolve away —

 Fever'd his high conceit of such a bride,

Yet brought him to the meekness of a child :

Alas ! when passion is both meek and wild !

7

So once more he had wak'd and anguished

 A dreary night of love and misery ,

If Isabel's quick eye had not been wed

直到伊莎貝拉的孤寂的面頰

　　在玫瑰該盛開的地方黯然消損，

清瞿得像年輕的母親，當她低唱

　　各種樣的催眠曲，撫慰嬰兒的病痛：

「啊，她多麼難過！」他想，「儘管我不該，

　　可是我決意明白宣告我的愛情：

若果容顏透露了她的心事，我要吻乾

她的眼淚，至少這會逐開她的憂煩。」

在一個美好的清晨，他這樣決定了，

　　他的心整天都在怦怦地跳；

他暗中向心兒禱告，但願給他力量

　　使他能表白；但心中赤熱的浪潮

窒息了他的聲音，推延他的決定 ──

　　美麗的伊莎貝拉越是使他驕傲，

在她前面，他也就越靦腆如兒童，

可不是！當愛情又是柔順，又是沸騰！

於是，他又一次睜著眼挨過了

　　充滿相思與折磨的淒涼夜景，

假如說，伊莎貝爾的敏銳的目光

To every symbol on his forehead high ;
She saw it waxing very pale and dead,
    And straight all flush'd ; so, lisped tenderly,
"Lorenzo ! " — here she ceas'd her timid quest,
But in her tone and look he read the rest.

8

"O Isabella, I can half perceive
    That I may speak my grief into thine ear ;
If thou didst ever anything believe,
    Believe how I love thee, believe how near
My soul is to its doom : I would not grieve
    Thy hand by unwelcome pressing, would not fear
Thine eyes by gazing ; but I cannot live
Another night, and not my passion shrive.

9

"Love ! thou art leading me from wintry cold,
    Lady ! thou leadest me to summer clime,
And I must taste the blossoms that unfold
    In its ripe warmth this gracious morning time. "
So said, his erewhile timid lips grew bold,
    And poesied with hers in dewy rhyme :
Great bliss was with them, and great happiness
Grew, like a lusty flower in June's caress.

並沒有看清他額際的每一表徵，
至少她看到，那前額蒼白而呆滯，
　　她立刻紅了臉；於是，她充滿柔情，
囁嚅著：「羅倫左！」── 才開口便又停頓，
但從她的音容他讀出了她的詢問。

8

「啊，伊莎貝拉！我不能十分肯定
　　是否我該把我的悲哀說給你聽；
假如你曾有過信心，請相信吧：
　　我是多麼愛你，我的靈魂已臨近
它的末日：我不願以魯莽的緊握
　　使你的手難過，也不願使你的眼睛
因被注視而吃驚；可是啊，我怎能
活過另一夜晚，而不傾訴我的熱情！

9

「愛啊：請領我走出冬季的嚴寒，
　　姑娘！我要你引我到夏日的地方；
我必須嚐一嚐在那炎熱的氣候
　　開放的花朵，它開放著美好的晨光。」
說完，他先前怯懦的嘴唇變為勇敢，
　　便和她的嘴唇，像兩句詩，把韻押上：
他們陶醉在幸福裏，巨大的快樂
滋生著，像六月所撫愛的艷麗花朵。

10

Parting they seem'd to tread upon the air,

 Twin roses by the zephyr blown apart

Only to meet again more close, and share

 The inward fragrance of each other's heart.

She, to her chamber gone, a ditty fair

 Sang, of delicious love and honey'd dart ;

He with light steps went up a western hill,

And bade the sun farewell, and joy'd his fill.

11

All close they met again, before the dusk

 Had taken from the stars its pleasant veil,

All close they met, all eves, before the dusk

 Had taken from the stars its pleasant veil,

Close in a bower of hyacinth and musk,

 Unknown of any, free from whispering tale.

Ah ! better had it been for ever so,

Than idle ears should pleasure in their woe.

12

Were they unhappy then ? — It cannot be —

 Too many tears for lovers have been shed,

Too many sighs give we to them in fee,

10

分手時，他們好像走在半空中，
　　好像是被和風吹開的玫瑰兩朵，
這分離只為了更親密的相聚，
　　好使彼此內心的芬芳交互融合。
她回到她的臥房，口裏唱著小曲，
　　唱著甜蜜的愛和傷心的情歌；
而他呢，以輕捷的步子登上西山，
向太陽揮手告別，心頭充滿了喜歡。

11

他們重又秘密地相聚，趁暮色
　　還沒有拉開它的帷幕，露出星星；
他們每天秘密地相聚，趁暮色
　　還沒有拉開它的帷幕，露出星星；
藏在風信子和麝香的花蔭裏，
　　躲開了人迹和人們的竊竊議論。
啊，頂好是永遠如此，免得讓
好事的耳朵喜悅於他們的悲傷。

12

那麼，難道他們不快樂？ ── 不可能 ──
　　只怪過多的眼淚寄予了有情人，
我們對他們付出過多的嘆息，

Too much of pity after they are dead,
Too many doleful stories do we see,
    Whose matter in bright gold were best be read ;
Except in such a page where Theseus' spouse
Over the pathless waves towards him bows.

13

But, for the general award of love,
    The little sweet doth kill much bitterness ;
Though Dido silent is in under-grove,
    And Isabella's was a great distress,
Though young Lorenzo in warm Indian clove
    Was not embalm'd, this truth is not the less —
Even bees, the little almsmen of spring-bowers,
Know there is richest juice in poison-flowers.

14

With her two brothers this fair lady dwelt,
    Enriched from ancestral merchandize,
And for them many a weary hand did swelt
    In torched mines and noisy factories,
And many once proud-quiver'd loins did melt

在他們死後又給了過多的憐憫；
我們看到太多的哀情故事，其實
　　那內容最好以燦爛的金字標明；
除非是這一頁故事：隔著波浪
忒修斯的妻子枉然把丈夫盼望。*

13

是的，對愛情無需有過多的報酬，
　　一絲甜蜜就能抵消大量的苦澀；
儘管黛多**在密樹叢裏安息了，
　　伊莎貝拉忍受了巨大的波折，
儘管羅倫左沒有在印度苜蓿花下
　　安享美夢，這真理依舊顛撲不破：
連小小的蜜蜂，向春日的亭蔭求布施，
也知道有毒的花朵才最富於甜汁。

14

這美人和兩個哥哥住在一起
　　祖先給他們留下了無數財產；
在火炬照耀的礦坑，在喧騰的工廠，
　　多少疲勞的人為他們揮汗；
啊，多少一度佩掛箭筒的腰身

　* 據希臘神話，忒修斯是海神之子，藉阿里阿德涅的幫助殺死了妖魔，他將阿里阿德涅
　　帶至涅克索斯島上將她遺棄。「忒修斯的妻子」即指阿里阿德涅。
** 據羅馬神話，黛多愛上了漂流至迦太基的埃涅阿斯。埃涅阿斯以後照神的旨意離開迦
　　太基，黛多被棄自殺。

217

In blood from stinging whip ; — with hollow eyes
Many all day in dazzling river stood,
To take the rich-ored driftings of the flood.

15

For them the Ceylon diver held his breath,
    And went all naked to the hungry shark ;
For them his ears gush'd blood ; for them in death
    The seal on the cold ice with piteous bark
Lay full of darts ; for them alone did seethe
    A thousand men in troubles wide and dark :
Half-ignorant, they turn'd an easy wheel,
That set sharp racks at work, to pinch and peel.

16

Why were they proud ?   Because their marble founts
    Gush'd with more pride than do a wretch's tears ? —
Why were they proud ?   Because fair orange- mounts
    Were of more soft ascent than lazar stairs ? —
Why were they proud ?   Because red-lin'd accounts
    Were richer than the songs of Grecian years ? —
Why were they proud ? again we ask aloud,
Why in the name of Glory were they proud ?

為鞭子抽出了血，在血裏軟癱；
多少人整天茫然地站在激流裏，
為了把水中金銀礦的沙石提取。

15

錫蘭的潛水者為他們屏住呼吸，
　　赤裸著全身走近飢餓的鯨魚；
他的耳朵為他們湧著血；為他們，
　　海豹死在冰層上，全身悲慘的
射滿了箭；成千的人只為了他們
　　而煎熬在幽暗無邊的困苦裏：
他們悠遊著歲月，自己還不甚清楚：
他們是在開動絞盤，把人們剝皮割骨。

16

他們何必驕傲？　因為有大理石噴泉
　　比可憐蟲的眼淚流得更歡騰？
他們何必驕傲？　因為有美麗的橘架
　　比貧病者的台階*更易於攀登？
他們何必驕傲？　可是因為有紅格帳本
　　比希臘時代的詩歌更動聽？
他們何必驕傲？我們還要高聲詢問：
在榮譽底名下，他們有什麼值得夸矜？

---

* 《舊約》〈路加福音〉中記載，拉撒路整日坐在富人門口的台階上乞食，死後升到天堂，
富人則入了地獄。這裏「貧病者的台階」似即指此事。

Yet were these Florentines as self-retired

    In hungry pride and gainful cowardice,

As two close Hebrews in that land inspired,

    Paled in and vineyarded from beggar-spies ;

The hawks of ship-mast forests — the untired

    And pannier'd mules for ducats and old lies —

Quick cat's-paws on the generous stray-away, —

Great wits in Spanish, Tuscan, and Malay.

18

How was it these same ledger-men could spy

    Fair Isabella in her downy nest ?

How could they find out in Lorenzo's eye

    A straying from his toil ?   Hot Egypt's pest

Into their vision covetous and sly !

    How could these money-bags see east and west ? —

Yet so they did — and every dealer fair

Must see behind, as doth the hunted hare.

19

O eloquent and famed Boccaccio !

17

但這兩個佛羅稜薩商人卻自滿於

　　淫侈的虛榮和富豪者的懦弱，

像是聖城*的兩個吝嗇的猶太人，

　　他們把窮人當奸細一樣嚴防著；

他們是盤旋在船桅間的鷹，是馱不盡

　　金銀與古老謊騙的衣冠的馬騾；

會向異鄉人的錢袋迅速伸出貓爪，

對西班牙、塔斯干、馬來文一律通曉。

18

像這樣算帳的人們怎會窺察出

　　伊莎貝拉的溫柔鄉的秘密？

他們怎會看出羅倫左的眼睛

　　有什麼在分神？　讓埃及的瘟疫

撲進他們貪婪而狡獪的眼吧！

　　這種守財奴怎會處處看得詳細？──

但竟然如此，　──　就像被追趕的野兔，

凡是正經的商人都必左右環顧。

19

哦，才氣磅礡的、著名的薄伽丘！

* 指巴勒斯坦。

Of thee we now should ask forgiving boon,
And of thy spicy myrtles as they blow,
        And of thy roses amorous of the moon,
And of thy lilies, that do paler grow
        Now they can no more hear thy ghittern's tune,
For venturing syllables that ill beseem
The quiet glooms of such a piteous theme.

20

Grant thou a pardon here, and then the tale
        Shall move on soberly, as it is meet ;
There is no other crime, no mad assail
        To make old prose in modern rhyme more sweet :
But it is done — succeed the verse or fail —
        To honour thee, and thy gone spirit greet ;
To stead thee as a verse in English tongue,
An echo of thee in the north-wind sung.

21

These brethren having found by many signs
        What love Lorenzo for their sister had,
And how she lov'd him too, each unconfines
        His bitter thoughts to other, well nigh mad
That he, the servant of their trade designs,

現在，我們需要你慷慨的祝福，
　　請賜給我們盛開的番石榴香花

　　和玫瑰 ── 如此爲月光所愛撫；
賜給我們百合吧，它變得更蒼白
　　因爲不再聽到你的琴聲低訴，
請原諒這魯莽的辭句，它拙於
表現這段陰鬱而沉默的悲劇。

20

只要受到你原諒，這故事一定會
　　順利地開展下去，有條有理；
我雖然拙劣，卻沒有狂妄的意圖
　　想把古代文章化爲更美的韻律：
它之所以寫作 ── 無論好或壞 ──
　　只爲了敬仰你，對你的天靈致意；
只爲在英文詩中豎立你的風格，
好使北國的風中也迴蕩你的歌。

21

從很多徵象，這兄弟倆看出了
　　羅倫左對妹妹有多深的愛情，
而且妹妹也熱愛他，這使他們
　　彼此談論起來，感到異常憤恨：
因爲他，他們商務中的一名小卒，

Should in their sister's love be blithe and glad,
When 'twas their plan to coax her by degrees
To some high noble and his olive-trees.

22

And many a jealous conference had they,
  And many times they bit their lips alone,
Before they fix'd upon a surest way
  To make the youngster for his crime atone ;
And at the last, these men of cruel clay
  Cut Mercy with a sharp knife to the bone ;
For they resolved in some forest dim
To kill Lorenzo, and there bury him.

23

So on a pleasant morning, as he leant
  Into the sun-rise, o'er the balustrade
Of the garden-terrace, towards him they bent
  Their footing through the dews ; and to him said,
"You seem there in the quiet of content,
  Lorenzo, and we are most loth to invade
Calm speculation ; but if you are wise,
Bestride your steed while cold is in the skies.

竟然享有了自己胞妹的愛情，
而他們正謀劃怎樣勸誘她接受
一個富豪的貴族，和他的橄欖樹！*

22

有很多次，他們在嫉恨地商議，
　　有很多次，他們咬著自己的嘴唇，
終於想出了最可靠的辦法
　　要叫那年輕人爲他的罪過抵命；
這兩個凶狠的人啊，簡直是
　　用尖刀把聖靈割得碎骨粉身，
因爲他們決定，要在幽暗的樹林裏
殺死羅倫左，並且把他掩埋滅迹。

23

於是，在一個晴和的早晨，正當他
　　在園中倚著亭台上的欄杆
把身子探進晨曦裏，他們便走過
　　露水凝聚的草地，來到他面前：
「羅倫左啊，你像是正在享受
　　適意的恬靜，我們很不願擾亂
你平靜的思緒，可是，假如你高興，
騎上你的馬吧，趁天空還這麼冷。

---

* 在佛羅棱薩，富人多在自己的莊園種橄欖樹。這裏即指田產。

225

24

"To-day we purpose, ay, this hour we mount
    To spur three leagues towards the Apennine ;
Come down, we pray thee, ere the hot sun count
    His dewy rosary on the eglantine. "
Lorenzo, courteously as he was wont,
    Bow'd a fair greeting to these serpents' whine ;
And went in haste, to get in readiness,
With belt, and spur, and bracing huntsman's dress.

25

And as he to the court-yard pass'd along,
    Each third step did he pause, and listen'd oft
If he could hear his lady's matin-song,
    Or the light whisper of her footstep soft ;
And as he thus over his passion hung,
    He heard a laugh full musical aloft ;
When, looking up, he saw her features bright
Smile through an in-door lattice, all delight.

26

"Love, Isabel !" said he, " I was in pain
    Lest I should miss to bid thee a good morrow :
Ah! what if I should lose thee, when so fain

24

「今天，我們想，不，這一刻我們要
    騎馬向阿本奈山地走三哩遠；
請你下來吧，趁炎熱的太陽
    還沒有把野玫瑰的露珠數完。」
羅倫左，像他經常一樣的儒雅，
    躬一躬身，聽從了這蛇蠍的嗚咽，
便趕忙走去了，爲的是裝備停當：
扎上皮帶、馬刺，穿好獵人的服裝。

25

而當他向庭院走近的時候，
    每走到第三步，便停下來留意
是否能聽見他的姑娘的晨歌，
    或聽見她輕柔的腳步的低語；
於是，正當他在熱情中流連，
    他聽到嘹亮的笑聲來自空際：
他抬起頭來，看見她光輝的容顏
在窗格裏微笑，秀麗好似天仙。

26

「伊莎貝爾，我的愛！」他說，「我多苦，
    害怕來不及對你道一聲早安：
唉！連這三小時的分別的悲傷

I am to stifle all the heavy sorrow

Of a poor three hours' absence ? but we'll gain

Out of the amorous dark what day doth borrow.

Good bye ! I'll soon be back. " — "Good bye ! " said she : —

And as he went she chanted merrily.

27

So the two brothers and their murder'd man

Rode past fair Florence, to where Arno's stream

Gurgles through straiten'd banks, and still doth fan

Itself with dancing bulrush, and the bream

Keeps head against the freshets. Sick and wan

The brothers' faces in the ford did seem,

Lorenzo's flush with love. — They pass'd the water

Into a forest quiet for the slaughter.

28

There was Lorenzo slain and buried in,

There in that forest did his great love cease ;

Ah ! when a soul doth thus its freedom win,

It aches in loneliness — is ill at peace

As the break-covert blood-hounds of such sin :

They dipp'd their swords in the water, and did tease

Their horses homeward, with convulsed spur,

Each richer by his being a murderer.

我都無法抑制住，假如我竟然
失去你怎麼辦？可是，我們將會
　　從愛情的幽暗得到愛情的白天。
再見吧！我就回來，」「再見吧！」她說；——
當他走去時，她快樂地唱著歌。

27

於是，兄弟倆和他們謀殺的人
　　騎馬走出佛羅稜薩，到阿諾河；
到那河邊，河水流過狹窄的山谷，
　　以歡躍的蘆葦把自己搖擺著，
而鯽魚逆著水灘前行。　　兩兄弟
　　在涉過河時，臉上都蒼白失色，
羅倫左卻滿面是愛情的紅潤。
他們過了河，來到幽靜的樹林。

28

羅倫左就在那兒被殺害和掩埋，
　　就在那林中，結束了他無比的愛情；
噢，當一個靈魂這樣脫出軀殼，
　　它在孤寂中絞痛 —— 不能寧靜，
一如犯了這種罪惡的惡狗們：
　　他們把自己的劍在河裏洗淨，
就策馬回家，馬刺被踢得歪扭，
每人由於當了殺人犯而更富有。

229

29

They told their sister how, with sudden speed,
 Lorenzo had ta'en ship for foreign lands,
Because of some great urgency and need
 In their affairs, requiring trusty hands.
Poor Girl ! put on thy stifling widow's weed,
 And 'scape at once from Hope's accursed bands ;
To-day thou wilt not see him, nor to-morrow,
And the next day will be a day of sorrow.

30

She weeps alone for pleasures not to be ;
 Sorely she wept until the night came on,
And then, instead of love, O misery !
 She brooded o'er the luxury alone :
His image in the dusk she seem'd to see,
 And to the silence made a gentle moan,
Spreading her perfect arms upon the air,
And on her couch low murmuring "Where ? O where ?"

31

But Selfishness, Love's cousin, held not long
 Its fiery vigil in her single breast ;
She fretted for the golden hour, and hung

他們告訴妹妹，羅倫左如何

　　由於商務的急切需要和緊迫，

而他們又沒有別人可信靠，

　　便派了他匆匆搭船去往外國。

可憐的姑娘！披上你寡婦的哀服吧，

　　快逃開「希望」底該詛咒的枷鎖；

今天你看不見他，明天也不能，

再過一天你還得滿心是悲痛。

她獨自為了不再有的歡樂

　　而哭泣，直痛哭到夜色降臨；

而那時，唉！痛苦代替了熱戀，

　　她獨自一個人冥想著歡情：

在幽暗中，她彷彿看見他的影子，

　　她對寂靜輕輕地發出悲吟；

接著把美麗的兩臂向空中舉起，

在臥榻上喃喃著：「哪裏？哦，哪裏？」

但「自私」── 「愛情」的堂弟 ── 並不能

　　在她專一的胸中永遠點著火焰；

她原為期待黃金的一刻而焦躁，

Upon the time with feverish unrest —
Not long — for soon into her heart a throng
    Of higher occupants, a richer zest,
Came tragic ; passion not to be subdued,
And sorrow for her love in travels rude.

32

In the mid days of autumn, on their eves
    The breath of Winter comes from far away,
And the sick west continually bereaves
    Of some gold tinge, and plays a roundelay
Of death among the bushes and the leaves,
    To make all bare before he dares to stray
From his north cavern.   So sweet Isabel
By gradual decay from beauty fell,

33

Because Lorenzo came not.   Oftentimes
    She ask'd her brothers, with an eye all pale,
Striving to be itself, what dungeon climes
    Could keep him off so long ?   They spake a tale
Time after time, to quiet her.   Their crimes
    Came on them, like a smoke from Hinnom's vale ;

急切不安地挨過孤寂的時間 ──
但沒有許久 ── 她心上就來了

　較高貴的情思，更豐富的慾念；
來了悲劇：那是不能抑制的眞情，
是對她的戀人突然遠行的悲痛。

32

在仲秋的一些日子，每逢黃昏，

　從遠方就飄來了多底呼吸，
它逐漸給病懨的西天剝奪了

　金黃的色彩，並且奏出死之曲
在灌木叢間，在籔籔的葉子上；

　它要使一切凋落，然後才敢於
離開它北方的岩洞。　就這樣，
伊莎貝爾的美色逐漸萎謝、無光，

33

因爲羅倫左不曾回來。　常常地

　她問她的哥哥（她的一雙眼
因爲矜持而無光），是什麼鬼地方

　把他拘留這麼久？　爲了使她心安，
他們回回編個謊。　他們的罪惡

　像新諾谷中的煙*在心中迴旋；

---

* 新諾谷在耶路撒冷西南。據《編年史》記載，阿哈茲在新諾谷中把自己的兩個孩子活活
燒死，以祭莫洛屈；因此，新諾谷中的煙使他想到自己的罪惡。

And every night in dreams they groan'd aloud,
To see their sister in her snowy shroud.

34

And she had died in drowsy ignorance,
 But for a thing more deadly dark than all ;
It came like a fierce potion, drunk by chance,
 Which saves a sick man from the feather'd pall
For some few gasping moments ; like a lance,
 Waking an Indian from his cloudy hall
With cruel pierce, and bringing him again
Sense of the gnawing fire at heart and brain.

35

It was a vision. — In the drowsy gloom,
 The dull of midnight, at her couch's foot
Lorenzo stood, and wept : the forest tomb
 Had marr'd his glossy hair which once could shoot
Lustre into the sun, and put cold doom
 Upon his lips, and taken the soft lute
From his lorn voice, and past his loamed ears
Had made a miry channel for his tears.

36

Strange sound it was, when the pale shadow spake ;

234

啊，每一夜，他們都在夢裏悲鳴，
看見妹妹似乎裏在白色的屍衣中。

34

而她呀，也許到死都茫然無知，
　　要不是有一個最難測的東西：
它像是偶然飲下的強心的藥
　　使病危的人可以多一刻喘息，
不致立刻僵斃；它像是長矛
　　以殘酷的一刺使印度人脫離
雲霧中的樓閣，使他重又感到
一團火焰在心中和腦中嚙咬。

35

這就是夢景。　── 在深沉的午夜
　　和昏睡的幽暗裏，羅倫左站在
她的床邊，落著淚：林中的墳墓
　　把他的髮間一度閃爍的光彩
弄暗了；給他的嘴唇按上了
　　冰冷的毀滅；使他悽涼的聲帶
失去柔和的曲調；在他的泥頰上，
又割出一條細渠使眼淚流淌。

36

幽靈開口，發出奇怪的聲音，

For there was striving, in its piteous tongue,
To speak as when on earth it was awake,
    And Isabella on its music hung :
Languor there was in it, and tremulous shake,
    As in a palsied Druid's harp unstrung ;
And through it moan'd a ghostly under-song,
Like hoarse night-gusts sepulchral briars among.

37

Its eyes, though wild, were still all dewy bright
    With love, and kept all phantom fear aloof
From the poor girl by magic of their light,
    The while it did unthread the horrid woof
Of the late darken'd time, — the murderous spite
    Of pride and avarice, — the dark pine roof
In the forest, — and the sodden turfed dell,
Where, without any word, from stabs he fell.

38

Saying moreover, "Isabel, my sweet !
    Red whortle-berries droop above my head,
And a large flint-stone weighs upon my feet ;
    Around me beeches and high chestnuts shed
Their leaves and prickly nuts ; a sheep-fold bleat
    Comes from beyond the river to my bed :

因為它那可悲的舌頭很想要
發出它生前所慣用的口音，
　　伊莎貝拉細細地聽那聲調：
它彷彿老僧以麻木的手彈破琴，
　　不合音符，又似無力而飄搖；
就從那口裏，幽靈的歌曲在嗚咽，
像是夜風颯颯穿過陰森的荊棘間。

37

幽靈的眼睛雖然悲傷，卻仍舊
　　充滿愛情，露水一般地閃亮，
這明光奇異地逐開恐懼底暗影，
　　使可憐的少女能略帶安詳，
聆聽幽靈講起那恐怖的時刻 ──
　　那傲慢與貪婪、那謀殺的狂妄，──
松林的蔭蔽處，── 水草的窪地，
在那兒，他無言地被刺倒下去。

38

他還說，「伊莎貝爾啊，我的愛！
　　我的頭上懸有紅色的越橘果，
一塊巨大的磨石壓在我腳下；
　　還有山毛櫸和高大的栗樹，灑落
葉子和果實在我四周；對岸有
　　羊群的咩叫從我榻上飄過：

237

Go, shed one tear upon my heather-bloom,
And it shall comfort me within the tomb.

39

"I am a shadow now, alas ! alas !
    Upon the skirts of human-nature dwelling
Alone : I chant alone the holy mass,
    While little sounds of life are round me knelling,
And glossy bees at noon do fieldward pass,
    And many a chapel bell the hour is telling,
Paining me through : those sounds grow strange to me,
And thou art distant in Humanity.

40

"I know what was, I feel full well what is,
    And I should rage, if spirits could go mad ;
Though I forget the taste of earthly bliss,
    That paleness warms my grave, as though I had
A Seraph chosen from the bright abyss
    To be my spouse : thy paleness makes me glad ;
Thy beauty grows upon me, and I feel
A greater love through all my essence steal. "

41

The Spirit mourn'd "Adieu!" — dissolv'd, and left

去吧，對我頭上的野花灑一滴淚，
那將使我在墳墓中得到安慰。

39

「唉，天哪！我如今是個影子了！
　　我獨自在人性的居室外邊
徘徊，獨自唱著謝主的彌撒，
　　聽生命的音響在我周身迴旋；
光澤的蜜蜂日午飛往田野，
　　多少教堂的鐘聲在報告時間；
這些聲音刺痛我，似熟而又陌生，
而你卻是遠遠的，處於人世中。

40

「我記得過去，對一切都有感覺，
　　哦，我必發瘋，如若我不是魂魄；
雖然我丟了人間幸福，那餘味
　　卻溫暖了我的墓穴，彷彿我
從光明的蒼穹有了一位天使
　　作為妻子；你的蒼白使我歡樂；
我漸漸愛上你的美色，我感到
更崇高的愛情在我魂中繚繞。」

41

幽靈呻吟道：「別了！」── 接著消隱，

The atom darkness in a slow turmoil;
As when of healthful midnight sleep bereft,
    Thinking on rugged hours and fruitless toil,
We put our eyes into a pillowy cleft,
    And see the spangly gloom froth up and boil :
It made sad Isabella's eyelids ache,
And in the dawn she started up awake ;

42

"Ha! ha!" said she, "I knew not this hard life,
    I thought the worst was simple misery ;
I thought some Fate with pleasure or with strife
    Portion'd us — happy days, or else to die ;
But there is crime — a brother's bloody knife !
    Sweet Spirit, thou hast school'd my infancy :
I'll visit thee for this, and kiss thine eyes,
And greet thee morn and even in the skies. "

43

When the full morning came, she had devised
    How she might secret to the forest hie ;
How she might find the clay, so dearly prized,
    And sing to it one latest lullaby ;
How her short absence might be unsurmised,
    While she the inmost of the dream would try.

給幽暗的空氣留下輕輕騷動；
好像當我們在午夜不能安眠，

　　想到艱難的經歷，無益的苦辛，
我們會把眼睛埋進枕頭縫隙，

　　看見閃爍的幽暗在翻動、沸騰：
悲哀的伊莎貝拉正是感到眼皮痛，
天剛破曉，她忽地坐起，睜開眼睛。

42

「哈哈！」她說，「誰懂得這冷酷的人生？

　　我曾以為最壞的不過是災難，
我以為命運只使人快樂或掙扎，

　　不是活得愉快，就是一命歸天；
想不到有罪惡，── 有哥哥的血刃！

　　親愛的幽靈啊，你教我變為成年：
為了這，我要去看你，吻你的眼，
每早每晚在天空中向你問安。」

43

在天光大亮時，她已盤算好

　　怎樣可以秘密地到樹林裏去；
怎樣可以找到那珍貴的泥土，

　　就對它唱一支最近的安眠曲；
怎樣使她的暫別不為人知道，

　　好把她內心的夢景加以證實。

Resolv'd, she took with her an aged nurse,
And went into that dismal forest-hearse.

44

See, as they creep along the river side,
How she doth whisper to that aged Dame,
And, after looking round the champaign wide,
Shows her a knife. — "What feverous hectic flame
Burns in thee, child ? — What good can thee betide,
That thou should'st smile again ? " — The evening came,
And they had found Lorenzo's earthy bed ;
The flint was there, the berries at his head.

45

Who hath not loiter'd in a green church-yard,
And let his spirit, like a demon-mole,
Work through the clayey soil and gravel hard,
To see scull, coffin'd bones, and funeral stole ;
Pitying each form that hungry Death hath marr'd,
And filling it once more with human soul ?
Ah! this is holiday to what was felt
When Isabella by Lorenzo knelt.

46

She gaz'd into the fresh-thrown mould, as though

決定以後，她就帶了老乳媽一人，
走進那陰森的靈棺似的樹林。

44

看啊，她們沿著河邊悄悄走去，
　　她不斷地對那老婆婆低語；
在環顧曠野以後，她拿出了
　　一柄刀。——「是什麼烈火在你心裏，
我的孩子？——究竟有什麼好事
　　又使你笑起來？」—— 暮色在凝聚；
她們找到了羅倫左的睡鄉：
那兒有磨石，有越橘樹在頭上。

45

誰不曾徘徊在青青的墳場，
　　讓自己的精靈，像一隻小鼴鼠，
穿過黏土的地層，堅硬的沙石，
　　去窺視腦殼、屍衣、棺中的枯骨？
誰不曾憐憫過那被飢餓的「死亡」
　　所蠶食的形體，想看它再次恢復
人的心靈？唉！這感覺卻不算悽慘，
比不得伊莎貝拉跪在羅倫左之前！

46

她凝視著那一抔新土，彷彿

243

One glance did fully all its secrets tell ;
Clearly she saw, as other eyes would know
    Pale limbs at bottom of a crystal well ;
Upon the murderous spot she seem'd to grow,
    Like to a native lily of the dell :
Then with her knife, all sudden, she began
To dig more fervently than misers can.

47

Soon she turn'd up a soiled glove, whereon
    Her silk had play'd in purple phantasies,
She kiss'd it with a lip more chill than stone,
    And put it in her bosom, where it dries
And freezes utterly unto the bone
    Those dainties made to still an infant's cries :
Then 'gan she work again ; nor stay'd her care,
But to throw back at times her veiling hair.

48

That old nurse stood beside her wondering,
    Until her heart felt pity to the core
At sight of such a dismal labouring,

只一瞥已完全看出它的隱秘；
　她清楚地看出來，清楚得像在
　　明亮的井中認出蒼白的肢體；
　她完全呆住在這謀殺的場所，
　　好似百合花扎根在幽谷裏：
突然，她拿起小刀往地下掘，
她掘得比守財奴還更心切。

47

她很快就挖出一只髒手套，
　那上面有她繡出的紫色幻想，
她吻著它，嘴唇比青石還冰冷，
　接著又把它放在她的心胸上，
就在那兒，它凍結了一切能止住
　嬰兒哭嚷的甘蜜，和她的幻想；＊
於是她又放手去掘，不稍間斷，
只有時把遮面的髮撩到後邊。

48

老乳媽站在一旁，奇怪地望著；
　這悽涼的景象，這墓穴的掘挖，
使她的心深處充滿了憐憫；

＊ 這句話比較難懂，因為太緊縮了內容。其意似為：伊莎貝拉作妻子和母親的幻想（類如
給嬰兒吃糖，使他不要哭泣等美好的幻景），都被這一只手套（象徵羅倫左的死）所摧毀
了。此處形象的美麗和含蓄，曾為批評家所稱讚。「她的幻想」一詞，尚是譯者所加
的。

And so she kneeled, with her locks all hoar,
And put her lean hands to the horrid thing :
    Three hours they labour'd at this travail sore ;
At last they felt the kernel of the grave,
And Isabella did not stamp and rave.

49

Ah! wherefore all this wormy circumstance ?
    Why linger at the yawning tomb so long ?
O for the gentleness of old Romance,
    The simple plaining of a minstrel's song !
Fair reader, at the old tale take a glance,
    For here, in truth, it doth not well belong
To speak : — O turn thee to the very tale,
And taste the music of that vision pale.

50

With duller steel than the Perséan sword
    They cut away no formless monster's head,
But one, whose gentleness did well accord
    With death, as life.   The ancient harps have said,
Love never dies, but lives, immortal Lord :
    If Love impersonate was ever dead,

於是她跪下來，披散一頭白髮，
用她枯柴的手也盡力幫著

　　做這可怕的工作；她們直向地下
掘了三點鐘，終於把墓穴摸到，
伊莎貝拉既不頓足，也不哭嚎。

49

噫！爲什麼盡是這陰森的描述？

　　爲什麼這支筆把墓門說個不完？
古老的傳奇故事是多麼文雅！

　　想想行吟的歌，那單純的哀怨！
親愛的讀者，還是請你讀一讀

　　原來的小說吧，因爲，在本篇
它實在講得不夠好：讀讀原作，
聽樂音如何流貫那暗淡的景色。

50

她們的鋼刀不及珀耳修斯的劍，*

　　割下的頭也不是畸形的魔妖，
而是這樣一個人，他死後依然優雅，

　　有如生時。　古代的豎琴曾唱道：
愛情不朽，它是主宰我們的神；

　　但它也許是化成肉身，而且死了，

---

* 希臘神話：珀耳修斯是大神宙斯之子，他殺死並割下了墨杜薩的頭。墨杜薩三姊妹原是
刀槍不入的，她們凝視誰，誰便會變成石頭。

247

Pale Isabella kiss'd it, and low moan'd.
'Twas love ; cold, — dead indeed, but not dethroned.

51

In anxious secrecy they took it home,
    And then the prize was all for Isabel :
She calm'd its wild hair with a golden comb,
    And all around each eye's sepulchral cell
Pointed each fringed lash ; the smeared loam
    With tears, as chilly as a dripping well,
She drench'd away : — and still she comb'd, and kept,
Sighing all day — and still she kiss'd, and wept.

52

Then in a silken scarf, — sweet with the dews
    Of precious flowers pluck'd in Araby,
And divine liquids come with odorous ooze
    Through the cold serpent-pipe refreshfully, —
She wrapp'd it up ; and for its tomb did choose
    A garden-pot, wherein she laid it by,
And cover'd it with mould, and o'er it set
Sweet Basil, which her tears kept ever wet.

53

And she forgot the stars, the moon, and sun,

伊莎貝拉正是吻著這肉身傷悲。
這正是愛情；啊，死了 ── 卻沒有退位。

51

她們急急把它秘密地帶回家，
　　於是它成了伊莎貝爾的寶藏：
她用金梳子梳著它散亂的頭髮，
　　又在每隻眼睛的陰森孔穴旁
把睫毛梳直；她以眼淚（它冰冷得
　　像石穴的水滴）把泥污的臉龐
洗拭乾淨： ── 她一面梳，一面嘆息，
整天不是吻著它，就是哭泣。

52

以後她用一方絲巾（它因有
　　阿拉伯的奇花的露水而香甜，
並且沾有各種神異的花汁，
　　彷彿剛從那幽冷的脈莖湧現，）
把它包裹了；又找出一個花盆
　　當做墳墓，就把它放在裏面；
於是她鋪上泥土，把一株紫蘇花
種植下去，用她的淚水不斷澆灑。

53

從此，她忘了日月和星辰，

249

And she forgot the blue above the trees,
And she forgot the dells where waters run,
    And she forgot the chilly autumn breeze ;
She had no knowledge when the day was done,
    And the new morn she saw not : but in peace
Hung over her sweet Basil evermore,
And moisten'd it with tears unto the core.

54

And so she ever fed it with thin tears,
    Whence thick, and green, and beautiful it grew,
So that it smelt more balmy than its peers
    Of Basil-tufts in Florence ; for it drew
Nurture besides, and life, from human fears,
    From the fast mouldering head there shut from view :
So that the jewel, safely casketed,
Came forth, and in perfumed leafits spread.

55

O Melancholy, linger here awhile !
    O Music, Music, breathe despondingly !
O Echo, Echo, from some sombre isle,
    Unknown, Lethean, sigh to us — O sigh !
Spirits in grief, lift up your heads, and smile ;
    Lift up your heads, sweet Spirits, heavily,

從此，她忘了樹梢上的青天，
她忘了流水潺潺的山谷，
　　也忘了冷峭的秋風飛旋；
她不再知道白天幾時消逝，
　　也看不見晨光升起，只不斷
靜靜地望著她甜蜜的紫蘇，
並且把淚水滴滴向它灌注。

54

就這樣，由於她的清淚的灌漑，
　　它繁茂地滋長，青綠而美麗；
它比佛羅稜薩所有的紫蘇花
　　都更芬芳，因爲它還從人所怕的
吸取到營養和生命，還從那
　　掩覆著的、迅速腐蝕的頭顱裏；
所以，這珍寶就從密封的盆中
開出花來，又把嫩葉伸到半空。

55

唉，憂鬱！在這兒稍停一會吧！
　　哦，樂音，樂音，請哀哀地呼吸！
還有回聲，回聲，請從渺茫的
　　忘川的島嶼 ── 對我們太息！
悲傷底精靈，抬起頭來，微笑吧；
　　精靈啊，把你們沉重的頭抬起，

And make a pale light in your cypress glooms,

Tinting with silver wan your marble tombs.

56

Moan hither, all ye syllables of woe,

    From the deep throat of sad Melpomene !

Through bronzed lyre in tragic order go,

    And touch the strings into a mystery ;

Sound mournfully upon the winds and low ;

    For simple Isabel is soon to be

Among the dead :   She withers, like a palm

Cut by an Indian for its juicy balm.

57

O leave the palm to wither by itself ;

    Let not quick Winter chill its dying hour ! —

It may not be — those Baälites of pelf,

    Her brethren, noted the continual shower

From her dead eyes ; and many a curious elf,

    Among her kindred, wonder'd that such dower

Of youth and beauty should be thrown aside

By one mark'd out to be a Noble's bride.

58

And, furthermore, her brethren wonder'd much

在這柏樹的幽暗中閃一閃亮，
把你們的石墓染上銀白的光。

56

到這兒呻吟啊，所有的哀辭，
　　請你們離開悲劇女神的喉嚨，
從青銅的豎琴上悒鬱而行，
　　把琴絃點化爲神秘的樂聲；
請對輕風悲哀而低迴地唱，
　　因爲啊，眞純的伊莎貝爾已不能
活得很久了：她枯萎有如那芭蕉：
印度人要爲了香汁把它砍掉。

57

啊，任由芭蕉自己去枯萎吧；
　　別再讓嚴多冷徹它臨終的一刻！——
也許不會 —— 但她那膜拜金錢的
　　哥哥，卻看到她呆枯的眼睛灑落
不斷的淚雨；不少好事的親友
　　也在奇怪，爲什麼在她將要充作
貴族的新娘的時候，卻不惜
將大好靑春與美底天賦委棄。

58

而且，更使她的哥哥詫異的是，

Why she sat drooping by the Basil green,
And why it flourish'd, as by magic touch ;
　　Greatly they wonder'd what the thing might mean :
They could not surely give belief, that such
　　A very nothing would have power to wean
Her from her own fair youth, and pleasures gay,
And even remembrance of her love's delay.

59

Therefore they watch'd a time when they might sift
　　This hidden whim ; and long they watch'd in vain ;
For seldom did she go to chapel-shrift,
　　And seldom felt she any hunger-pain ;
And when she left, she hurried back, as swift
　　As bird on wing to breast its eggs again ;
And, patient as a hen-bird, sat her there
Beside her Basil, weeping through her hair.

60

Yet they contriv'd to steal the Basil-pot,
　　And to examine it in secret place :
The thing was vile with green and livid spot,
　　And yet they knew it was Lorenzo's face :
The guerdon of their murder they had got,
　　And so left Florence in a moment's space,

為什麼她總垂頭坐在紫蘇前，
為什麼花兒盛開，像具有魔力，
　這一切都給他們提出了疑難；
的確，他們不能相信，這一盆
　渺不足道的東西，竟能截斷
她美好的青春，竊取她的歡愉，
甚至霸佔她戀人遠行的記憶。

59

所以，他們觀察許久，想解答
　這一個啞謎；但都歸枉然；
因為她很少到教堂去懺悔，
　也很少感到飢餓的熬煎；
她每次離房，都很快就回來，
　好像飛開的鳥要回來孵卵；
她也和雌鳥一樣耐心，面對著
她的紫蘇，任淚珠朝髮絲滾落。

60

但他們終於偷到了紫蘇花盆，
　並且把它拿到暗地裏仔細考察：
他們看到青綠而灰白的一物，
　正是羅倫左的臉，分毫不差！
啊，他們終於得到了謀殺底報酬：
　兩人匆匆離開了佛羅稜薩，

Never to turn again. — Away they went,
With blood upon their heads, to banishment.

61

O Melancholy, turn thine eyes away !
        O Music, Music, breathe despondingly !
O Echo, Echo, on some other day,
        From isles Lethean, sigh to us — O sigh !
Spirits of grief, sing not your "Well-a-way ! "
        For Isabel, sweet Isabel, will die ;
Will die a death too lone and incomplete,
Now they have ta'en away her Basil sweet.

62

Piteous she look'd on dead and senseless things,
        Asking for her lost Basil amorously ;
And with melodious chuckle in the strings
        Of her lorn voice, she oftentimes would cry
After the Pilgrim in his wanderings,
        To ask him where her Basil was ; and why
'Twas hid from her : "For cruel 'tis, " said she,
"To steal my Basil-pot away from me. "

63

And so she pined, and so she died forlorn,

從此不再回來。 ── 他們的頭上
戴著血罪，從此流落在異鄉。

61

唉，憂鬱！移開你的視線吧！
　　哦，樂音，樂音，請哀哀地呼吸！
還有回聲，回聲，請在另一天
　　從你的忘川之島對我們太息！
悲傷底精靈啊，暫停你的喪歌，
　　因為甜蜜的伊莎貝爾將死去；
她將死得不稱心，死得孤獨，
因為他們奪走了她的紫蘇。

62

可憐的她望著無感覺的木石，
　　儘向它們追問她失去的紫蘇；
每看到遊方的僧人，她就帶著
　　悽苦而清朗的笑聲向他招呼，
並且問道，為什麼人們把她的
　　紫蘇花隱藏起來了，藏在何處；
「因為啊，」她說，「是誰這麼殘忍，
竟偷去了我的紫蘇花盆。」

63

就這樣，她憔悴，她孤寂地死去，

Imploring for her Basil to the last.
No heart was there in Florence but did mourn
    In pity of her love, so overcast.
And a sad ditty of this story born
    From mouth to mouth through all the country pass'd :
Still is the burthen sung — "O cruelty,
To steal my Basil-pot away from me ! "

直到死前，總把紫蘇問個不停。

佛羅稜薩沒有一顆心不難過，

　　不對她的哀情表示憐憫。

有人把這故事編成了一支

　　悽涼的歌曲，這曲子傳遍全城；

它的尾聲仍舊是：「啊，太殘忍！

誰竟偷去了我的紫蘇花盆！」

　　　　　　　　　　　1818年2月

The Eve of St. Agnes

1

S T. AGNES' Eve — Ah, bitter chill it was !
    The owl, for all his feathers, was a-cold ;
The hare limp'd trembling through the frozen grass,
And silent was the flock in woolly fold :
Numb were the Beadsman's fingers, while he told
His rosary, and while his frosted breath,
Like pious incense from a censer old,
Seem'd taking flight for heaven, without a death,
Past the sweet Virgin's picture, while his prayer he saith.

2

His prayer he saith, this patient, holy man ;
Then takes his lamp, and riseth from his knees,
And back returneth, meagre, barefoot, wan,
Along the chapel aisle by slow degrees :
The sculptur'd dead, on each side, seem to freeze,
Emprison'd in black, purgatorial rails :

聖亞尼節的前夕 *

1

聖亞尼節的前夕 —— 多麼冷峭！
夜梟的羽毛雖厚，也深感嚴寒；
兔兒顫抖著瘸過冰地的草，
羊欄裏的綿羊都噤若寒蟬；
誦經人的手凍僵了，拿著念珠，
嘴裏不斷禱告；他呵出的氣
像古爐中焚燒的香，凝成白霧，
彷彿向天庭飛升，不稍停息，
娓娓直抵聖母的畫像，又飛上去。

2

把禱告作完了，這耐心的僧侶
便拿起燈盞，抬起雙膝，赤著腳，
他蒼白而清瞿的，緩緩走去，
重又走上教堂座間的夾道；
在兩旁，死者的雕像好似凍住
在那黑色的、淨獄界的圍欄中；

---

* 聖亞尼是羅馬少女，於十四歲時以身殉基督教。聖亞尼節的前夕在一月二十日，傳說在這一夜，少女在進行禱告後可以夢見未來的丈夫。又：原詩每節的韻腳是121223233，譯詩稍有改變，是121234344。

Knights, ladies, praying in dumb orat'ries,
He passeth by ; and his weak spirit fails
To think how they may ache in icy hoods and mails.

3

Northward he turneth through a little door,
And scarce three steps, ere Music's golden tongue
Flatter'd to tears this aged man and poor ;
But no — already had his deathbell rung :
The joys of all his life were said and sung :
His was harsh penance on St. Agnes' Eve :
Another way he went, and soon among
Rough ashes sat he for his soul's reprieve,
And all night kept awake, for sinners' sake to grieve.

4

That ancient Beadsman heard the prelude soft ;
And so it chanc'd, for many a door was wide,
From hurry to and fro.   Soon, up aloft,
The silver, snarling trumpets 'gan to chide :
The level chambers, ready with their pride,
Were glowing to receive a thousand guests :
The carved angels, ever eager-eyed,
Star'd, where upon their heads the cornice rests,
With hair blown back, and wings put cross-wise on their breasts.

騎士、淑女，都正在默默地跪伏，
　　他走過去，也無心去想他們
披著甲冑和披肩，不知怎樣僵痛。

3

　　他向北走，從一扇小門走出，
　　還不到三步，清婉樂音的金舌
　　就把蒼邁老僧的眼淚勾出；
　　唉，夠了！── 他的喪鐘早已敲過；
　　他此生的歡樂已經數盡、唱完：
　　在聖亞尼節的前夕，只有懺悔
　　是他的份：他換條路走，轉瞬間
　　他已坐在灰堆上替靈魂贖罪，
也為了造孽的世人，整夜在心悲。

4

　　老僧人所以聽到委婉的前奏，
　　這是因為，很多人來來往往
　　使門戶透進了樂曲。　而不久
　　銀鈴般刺耳的號聲開始激蕩：
　　一排房間被燈火照得通明
　　等著接待成千的賓客：許多天使
　　雕刻在飛檐下面，都睜大眼睛
　　永遠向著上空熱烈地注視，
頭髮往後飄揚，胸前交迭著雙翅。

263

5

At length burst in the argent revelry,

With plume, tiara, and all rich array,

Numerous as shadows haunting fairily

The brain, new stuff'd, in youth, with triumphs gay

Of old romance.   These let us wish away,

And turn, sole-thoughted, to one Lady there,

Whose heart had brooded, all that wintry day,

On love, and wing'd St. Agnes' saintly care,

As she had heard old dames full many times declare.

6

They told her how, upon St. Agnes' Eve,

Young virgins might have visions of delight,

And soft adorings from their loves receive

Upon the honey'd middle of the night,

If ceremonies due they did aright ;

As, supperless to bed they must retire,

And couch supine their beauties, lily white ;

Nor look behind, nor sideways, but require

Of Heaven with upward eyes for all that they desire.

7

Full of this whim was thoughtful Madeline :

終於，輝煌的盛會開始了，
到處是毛羽、冠冕、盛裝與銀飾，
燦爛得彷彿少年人的思潮：
無數幻影和古代傳奇的韻事
都在那裏聚集。　但撇開閒言，
且讓我們敘說有一個少女：
啊，那整個冬季，她的心不斷
　冥想著愛情，想著聖亞尼天使，
因為老乳媼對她講過了很多次。

乳媼說，在聖亞尼節的前夕，
姑娘們都能看到戀人的影相，
只要她們遵守正確的儀式，
在甜蜜的午夜，她們的情郎
就會在夢中對她們情話綿綿；
她們必須不吃晚餐就上床，
將百合似的玉體仰臥朝天，
　不准斜視或後顧，只面對天堂，
只對上天默念她們的一切願望。

梅德琳的腦中充滿這幻想：

The music, yearning like a God in pain,

She scarcely heard : her maiden eyes divine,

Fix'd on the floor, saw many a sweeping train

Pass by — she heeded not at all : in vain

Came many a tiptoe, amorous cavalier,

And back retir'd ; not cool'd by high disdain,

But she saw not : her heart was otherwhere :

She sigh'd for Agnes' dreams, the sweetest of the year.

8

She danc'd along with vague, regardless eyes,

Anxious her lips, her breathing quick and short :

The hallow'd hour was near at hand : she sighs

Amid the timbrels, and the throng'd resort

Of whisperers in anger, or in sport ;

'Mid looks of love, defiance, hate, and scorn,

Hoodwink'd with faery fancy ; all amort,

Save to St. Agnes and her lambs unshorn,

And all the bliss to be before to-morrow morn.

9

So, purposing each moment to retire,

She linger'd still.   Meantime, across the moors,

樂聲雖高，像天神痛苦的呻吟，
她卻沒聽見；仕女熙熙攘攘
行經她跟前，但她虔誠的眼睛
只垂向地板，絲毫不曾看到。
多少鍾情少年朝她踮腳走來
又悄悄退回；並不是她驕傲，
而是看不見：啊，她的心早已不在，
爲了聖亞尼的夢，飛往九霄雲外。

8

她淡漠而茫然地和人舞蹈，
唇乾舌燥，呼吸短促而迫急：
莊嚴的時辰快到了，她直心跳，
既聽不見鼓聲，也無意擁擠
去與人憤慨地低語，或者說笑；
愛與恨、無禮與輕蔑的世相
都被幻想蔽住，不再使她看到，
除了聖亞尼和她的一群羔羊，*
還有午夜的歡樂在眼前蕩漾。

9

就這般，她耽延著，每一刻
都想走開。　但這時，馳過荒原，

* 聖亞尼的祭祀時，必使用羔羊。

267

Had come young Porphyro, with heart on fire

For Madeline.   Beside the portal doors,

Buttress'd from moonlight, stands he, and implores

All saints to give him sight of Madeline,

But for one moment in the tedious hours,

That he might gaze and worship all unseen ;

Perchance speak, kneel, touch, kiss — in sooth such things have been.

10

He ventures in : let no buzz'd whisper tell :

All eyes be muffled, or a hundred swords

Will storm his heart, Love's fev'rous citadel :

For him, those chambers held barbarian hordes,

Hyena foemen, and hot-blooded lords,

Whose very dogs would execrations howl

Against his lineage : not one breast affords

Him any mercy, in that mansion foul,

Save one old beldame, weak in body and in soul.

11

Ah, happy chance ! the aged creature came,

Shuffling along with ivory-headed wand,

To where he stood, hid from the torch's flame,

Behind a broad hall-pillar, far beyond

The sound of merriment and chorus bland :

少年波菲羅心　滿是情火，
朝梅德琳來了。　他立於門邊
守在月陰處，暗向聖徒禱告：
但願得見梅德琳，哪怕是等它
漫長的幾點鐘，只要能悄悄
注視她一會，甚或還對她談話，
下跪，接觸、親吻 —— 膜拜一剎那。

10

他側身走進來：唉，千萬可藏好，
誰也不准看見，要不然，百把劍
就刺穿他的心，那愛情的碉堡；
對他說，這裏好似一夥生番，
是鬣狗似的仇敵，憤怒的暴君，
連他們的狗都會對他的門楣
吠出詛咒。他們沒有一個人
對他心懷仁慈；整個爵府內，
只有一個老嫗能以笑顏相對。

11

啊，巧得很！正是那老嫗來了，
拄著象牙頭的拐杖，蹣蹣跚跚；
他站腳的地方，火炬照不到，
又擋在門柱後為人所不見，
也遠離歡笑與嘈雜的喧聲：

He startled her ; but soon she knew his face,

And grasp'd his fingers in her palsied hand,

Saying, "Mercy, Porphyro ! hie thee from this place ;

They are all here to-night, the whole blood-thirsty race !

12

"Get hence ! get hence ! there's dwarfish Hildebrand ;

He had a fever late, and in the fit

He cursed thee and thine, both house and land :

Then there's that old Lord Maurice, not a whit

More tame for his gray hairs — Alas me ! flit !

Flit like a ghost away. " — "Ah, Gossip dear,

We're safe enough ; here in this arm-chair sit,

And tell me how" — "Good Saints ! not here, not here ;

Follow me, child, or else these stones will be thy bier. "

13

He follow'd through a lowly arched way,

Brushing the cobwebs with his lofty plume,

And as she mutter'd "Well-a—well-a-day ! "

He found him in a little moonlight room,

Pale, lattic'd, chill, and silent as a tomb.

"Now tell me where is Madeline, " said he,

"O tell me, Angela, by the holy loom

Which none but secret sisterhood may see,

老嫗猛吃一驚，但立刻認出了
是他，便把他的手握在手中，
　說道：「天啊，波菲羅！快快逃跑；
他們全在這兒，誰見你也不饒！

12

「快走！快走！矮子西爾得勃蘭
最近生過熱病，病中還咒罵
你和你的一族，你整個的家園；
莫理斯爵爺雖然是一頭白髮，
也對你心懷不善 ── 唉！跑吧！
跑得無影無蹤。」──「不，老婆婆，
　這兒足夠安全的；你且坐下，
告訴我 ──」「天哪！別在這，別在這；
跟我來，孩子，不然你免不了災禍。」

13

他跟著她，穿過低矮的走廊，
他的纓毛擦過了蛛網灰塵，
來到一間小屋，屋裏有月光
從窗格透進來，蒼白、寂靜、陰森，
有如墳墓。老嫗這才把心鬆開。
「現在告訴我吧，」他說，「哪兒是
　梅德琳呀？噢，告訴我，請看在
那神聖的織機面上（只有修女

271

When they St. Agnes' wool are weaving piously. "

14

"St. Agnes ! Ah ! it is St. Agnes' Eve —
Yet men will murder upon holy days :
Thou must hold water in a witch's sieve,
And be liege-lord of all the Elves and Fays,
To venture so : it fills me with amaze
To see thee, Porphyro ! — St. Agnes' Eve !
God's help ! my lady fair the conjuror plays
This very night : good angels her deceive !
But let me laugh awhile, I've mickle time to grieve. "

15

Feebly she laugheth in the languid moon,
While Porphyro upon her face doth look,
Like puzzled urchin on an aged crone
Who keepeth clos'd a wond'rous riddle-book,
As spectacled she sits in chimney nook.
But soon his eyes grew brilliant, when she told
His lady's purpose ; and he scarce could brook
Tears, at the thought of those enchantments cold,
And Madeline asleep in lap of legends old.

在那上織出聖亞尼的絨衣）。」*

14

「呀，聖亞尼！這是聖亞尼前夕 ──
可是就在節期，人們還是殺戮：
除非你能叫篩裏的水不滴，
要不能把妖魔鬼怪都管住
怎敢到這裏？啊，你多叫我心驚，
波菲羅！ ── 竟在今晚跟你見面！
今晚呀，我的小姐要祭神明，
但求天使幫忙，把她騙一騙！
我要笑笑，傷心可有的是時間。」

15

她微弱的笑在月光裏蕩漾；
波菲羅儘望著老嫗的面孔，
彷彿是老婆婆坐在爐火旁
戴上眼鏡，而小頑童目不轉睛
望著她，等她講解一本奇書。
但一待她說出小姐的心意，
他雙目立刻灼亮，卻又忍不住
流下眼淚，想到在如此寒夜裏，
梅德琳要照古代的傳說安息。

---

* 在聖亞尼祭禮上使用的羔羊，經常取其毛，用特殊的織機織成布，作成衣服。此處波菲
羅就以這「神聖的織機」起誓。

273

16

Sudden a thought came like a full-blown rose,

Flushing his brow, and in his pained heart

Made purple riot : then doth he propose

A stratagem, that makes the beldame start :

"A cruel man and impious thou art :

Sweet lady, let her pray, and sleep, and dream

Alone with her good angels, far apart

From wicked men like thee.   Go, go ! — I deem

Thou canst not surely be the same that thou didst seem. "

17

"I will not harm her, by all saints I swear, "

Quoth Porphyro : "O may I ne' er find grace

When my weak voice shall whisper its last prayer,

If one of her soft ringlets I displace,

Or look with ruffian passion in her face :

Good Angela, believe me by these tears ;

Or I will, even in a moment' s space,

Awake, with horrid shout, my foemen' s ears,

And beard them, though they be more fang' d than wolves and bears. "

18

"Ah ! why wilt thou affright a feeble soul ?

突然有個念頭，像玫瑰花開，
紅透了他的鬢角，又在他心中
攪起一片紫波：而等他說出來
這個計謀，老婆婆卻吃一驚：
「呀，不料你這麼放肆、荒唐；
好姑娘，儘她自個去禱告、作夢、
和好天使作伴吧，千萬別讓
你這種壞人來打擾。　去去！　如今
我看你再也不像從前那麼好心。」

「我絕不驚擾她，啊，神明在上！」
波菲羅說，「如若我不守誓言，
動了她柔髮一絲，或對她面龐
投上無禮的一瞥，就讓老天
對我臨死的祈禱堵住耳朵：
好安吉拉啊，憑這眼淚，請相信
我的真誠吧，不然，就在此刻
我要大聲嚎叫，喚出我的仇人，
我要一拚，儘管他們比虎狼還凶。」

「咳！你何苦讓我這老命殘生

A poor, weak, palsy-stricken, churchyard thing,
Whose passing-bell may ere the midnight toll ;
Whose prayers for thee, each morn and evening,
Were never miss'd. " — Thus plaining, doth she bring
A gentler speech from burning Porphyro ;
So woful, and of such deep sorrowing,
That Angela gives promise she will do
Whatever he shall wish, betide her weal or woe.

19

Which was, to lead him, in close secrecy,
Even to Madeline's chamber, and there hide
Him in a closet, of such privacy
That he might see her beauty unespied,
And win perhaps that night a peerless bride,
While legion'd fairies pac'd the coverlet,
And pale enchantment held her sleepy-eyed.
Never on such a night have lovers met,
Since Merlin paid his Demon all the monstrous debt.

20

"It shall be as thou wishest, " said the Dame :
"All cates and dainties shall be stored there

跟著你擔驚受怕？黃泉不遠，
不到午夜就許敲出我的喪鐘；
還不是爲了你，我每天早晚
都默默禱告！」她說完這番話，
波菲羅立刻也放軟了語氣；
他是這麼難過、悲哀、心亂如麻，
安吉拉一口答應：她必盡力
幫助他，赴湯蹈火也在所不惜。

19

那就是，她要偷偷把他領到
小姐的閨房，把他藏在壁櫥裏，
這樣，他就可以從帷後悄悄
窺伺著美人，以稱他的心意。
而如果那一夜，有成隊的妖仙
舞於被面，使她的眼受到魔祟，
他也許就締結了美滿姻緣。
啊，自從莫林*將宿債償還了魔鬼，
還不見有情人今夕如此相會。

20

老婆婆說，「一切都依你的話。
我要快把糖果和糕點擺好：

* 莫林是一個老巫師，因爲將符咒給了一個邪惡的少女，少女反將他永遠閉鎖在一棵橡樹裏。詳見丁尼生（Tennyson, 1809—92）的《國王牧歌》。

Quickly on this feast-night : by the tambour frame
Her own lute thou wilt see : no time to spare,
For I am slow and feeble, and scarce dare
On such a catering trust my dizzy head.
Wait here, my child, with patience ; kneel in prayer
The while :   Ah ! thou must needs the lady wed,
Or may I never leave my grave among the dead. "

21

So saying, she hobbled off with busy fear.
The lover' s endless minutes slowly pass' d ;
The dame return' d, and whisper' d in his ear
To follow her ; with aged eyes aghast
From fright of dim espial.   Safe at last,
Through many a dusky gallery, they gain
The maiden' s chamber, silken, hush' d, and chaste ;
Where Porphyro took covert, pleas' d amain.
His poor guide hurried back with agues in her brain.

22

Her falt' ring hand upon the balustrade,
Old Angela was feeling for the stair,
When Madeline, St. Agnes' charmed maid,
Rose, like a mission' d spirit, unaware :
With silver taper' s light, and pious care,

她的琵琶就挨著刺繡繃架，
你就會看到。　哦，我可得去了；
你看我又老又慢，體力不支，
這擺席的大事可糊塗不得：
你且耐心等一會吧，我的孩子，
求求天：你和小姐一定能結合，
不然，就讓我死後魂無歸所。」

21

說完，她蹣跚地去了，滿心惶恐。
戀人的時光真漫長而遲緩；
老乳媼回來了，附在他耳中
說道，「跟我來吧」；她驚惶的老眼
生怕暗中有人，不住地張望；
他們穿過了許多陰森廊道，
走到少女幽靜的絲幃繡房，
波菲羅快活地在室內藏好，
他的嚮導也走開，腦中在發燒。

22

正當安吉拉的顫巍巍的手
扶著欄杆，在暗中摸索樓梯，
中魔似的梅德琳恰巧上樓
要來度過她聖亞尼的佳夕：
手執著銀燭，她轉頭將老婆婆

She turn'd, and down the aged gossip led
To a safe level matting.   Now prepare,
Young Porphyro, for gazing on that bed ;
She comes, she comes again, like ring-dove fray'd and fled.

23

Out went the taper as she hurried in ;
Its little smoke, in pallid moonshine, died :
She clos'd the door, she panted, all akin
To spirits of the air, and visions wide :
No uttered syllable, or, woe betide !
But to her heart, her heart was voluble,
Paining with eloquence her balmy side ;
As though a tongueless nightingale should swell
Her throat in vain, and die, heart-stifled, in her dell.

24

A casement high and triple-arch'd there was,
All garlanded with carven imag'ries
Of fruits, and flowers, and bunches of knot-grass,
And diamonded with panes of quaint device,
Innumerable of stains and splendid dyes,
As are the tiger-moth's deep-damask'd wings ;

小心扶下樓梯，扶到了平地上。
啊，現在，幸福的少年波菲羅：
準備好吧，快注視那一張繡床；
她來了，又來了，像飛鴿不斷迴翔。

23

她匆匆進來，燭火被風吹熄，
一縷清煙散入了銀灰的月光；
她閉起房門，心跳得多麼急，
啊，她已如此臨近仙靈和幻象：
別吐一個字，不然就大禍臨頭！*
可是啊，她的心卻充滿了言語，
一腔心事好似有骨鯁在喉；
有如一隻啞夜鶯唱不出歌曲，
只好窒悶於胸，鬱鬱死在谷裏。

24

三層弧形的窗櫺十分高大，
有精巧的花紋鏤刻在窗頂，
果實、枝葉和蘆草纏結垂掛；
窗心嵌著各種樣的玻璃水晶：
繽紛的五彩交織，奇光燦爛，
好像虎蛾的翅膀映輝似錦；

---

* 儀式的條件之一是，必須絕對緘默，才能在夢中看到情人。

281

And in the midst, 'mong thousand heraldries,

And twilight saints, and dim emblazonings,

A shielded scutcheon blush'd with blood of queens and kings.

25

Full on this casement shone the wintry moon,

And threw warm gules on Madeline's fair breast,

As down she knelt for heaven's grace and boon ;

Rose-bloom fell on her hands, together prest,

And on her silver cross soft amethyst,

And on her hair a glory, like a saint :

She seem'd a splendid angel, newly drest,

Save wings, for heaven : — Porphyro grew faint :

She knelt, so pure a thing, so free from mortal taint.

26

Anon his heart revives : her vespers done,

Of all its wreathed pearls her hair she frees ;

Unclasps her warmed jewels one by one ;

Loosens her fragrant boddice ; by degrees

Her rich attire creeps rustling to her knees :

Half-hidden, like a mermaid in sea-weed,

Pensive awhile she dreams awake, and sees,

In fancy, fair St. Agnes in her bed,

But dares not look behind, or all the charm is fled.

在這幽暗如層雲的花紋中間，
　在天使的陰蔽下，立著一面盾，
像被帝王和后妃的血所浸潤。

25

　寒冷的月色正投在這窗上，
　也在梅德琳的玉潔的前胸
　照出溫暖的絳紋；她正在合掌
　向天默禱，像有玫瑰覆落手中；
　她那銀十字變成了紫水晶，
　她的髮上閃著光輪，有如聖徒：
　又好似光輝的天使正待飛升，
　啊，波菲羅已看得神志恍惚：
她跪著，這麼純淨，似已超然無物。

26

　但他又心跳起來：晚禱完畢，
　她就除去髮間的珠簪和玉針，
　又將溫馨的寶石一一摘取；
　接著解開芳馥的胸兜，讓衣裙
　窸窣地輕輕滑落在她膝前，
　這使她半裸，像擁海藻的人魚；
　沉思了一會，她睜開夢幻的眼，
　彷彿她的床上就睡著聖亞尼，
但又不敢回身看，生怕幻象飛去。

27

Soon, trembling in her soft and chilly nest,

In sort of wakeful swoon, perplex'd she lay,

Until the poppied warmth of sleep oppress'd

Her soothed limbs, and soul fatigued away ;

Flown, like a thought, until the morrow- day ;

Blissfully haven' d both from joy and pain ;

Clasp' d like a missal where swart Paynims pray ;

Blinded alike from sunshine and from rain,

As though a rose should shut, and be a bud again.

28

Stol' n to this paradise, and so entranced,

Porphyro gazed upon her empty dress,

And listen' d to her breathing, if it chanced

To wake into a slumberous tenderness ;

Which when he heard, that minute did he bless,

And breath' d himself : then from the closet crept,

Noiseless as fear in a wide wilderness,

And over the hush'd carpet, silent, stept,

And ' tween the curtains peep'd, where, lo! — how fast she slept.

29

Then by the bed- side, where the faded moon

只片刻，她已朦朧不甚清醒，
微微抖顫在她寒冷的軟巢裏；
接著來了睡眠，以罌粟的溫馨
撫慰了她的四肢，讓神魂脫體
好似一縷柔思飛往夜空，
幸福的脫離了苦樂，緊緊閉住
像一本《聖經》在異教徒的手中；
不但忘卻陽光，也不沾雨露，
彷彿玫瑰花瓣開了、又能收束。

偷到了這天國，滿心是狂喜，
波菲羅儘望著她脫下的衣裙；
又細細聆聽，是否她的呼吸
已在睡神的溫柔鄉裏甦醒；
啊，確係如此；他謝過了神明，
舒了口氣，便躡足出了壁櫥，
像荒野中的恐懼，寂靜無聲；
他悄然走過地氈，輕踮著腳步，
掀開絲帷只一瞥：呀，她睡得多熟！

靠近床邊，正有暗淡的月光

Made a dim, silver twilight, soft he set
A table, and, half anguish'd, threw thereon
A cloth of woven crimson, gold, and jet : —
O for some drowsy Morphean amulet !
The boisterous, midnight, festive clarion,
The kettle- drum, and far- heard clarinet,
Affray his ears, though but in dying tone : —
The hall door shuts again, and all the noise is gone.

30

And still she slept an azure-lidded sleep,
In blanched linen, smooth, and lavender'd,
While he from forth the closet brought a heap
Of candied apple, quince, and plum, and gourd ;
With jellies soother than the creamy curd,
And lucent syrops, tinct with cinnamon ;
Manna and dates, in argosy transferr'd
From Fez ; and spiced dainties, every one,
From silken Samarcand to cedar'd Lebanon.

31

These delicates he heap'd with glowing hand
On golden dishes and in baskets bright

投下銀灰的朦朧，他就在那裏
輕輕放下桌子，又小心地鋪上
繡花桌布（硃赤、金黃兼墨玉）；
從遠處，午夜的宴會不斷傳來
喧騰的笑鬧聲、笙簫與鼓號：
噢，但願夢神的護符能隔開
這刺耳的雜音，儘管如此縹緲；
他關上了堂門，一切復歸靜悄。

30

她覆蓋著噴香的雪白被褥，
正安享爲藍眼瞼鎖住的睡眠；
波菲羅這時從櫥櫃裏搬出
蜜餞、蘋果、靑梅和木瓜多盤，
還有各種果醬，滑膩似乳酪，
透明的果子露含有肉桂味，
還有各種香糕，以及自摩洛哥
運來的蜜棗、仙果，無一不備，
無論是沙馬甘、*或黎巴嫩的珍貴。

31

這些珍品有的擺在金盤上，
有的盛以銀絲編就的筐籃，

* 舊時俄國地名。

Of wreathed silver : sumptuous they stand
In the retired quiet of the night,
Filling the chilly room with perfume light. —
"And now, my love, my seraph fair, awake !
Thou art my heaven, and I thine eremite :
Open thine eyes, for meek St. Agnes' sake,
Or I shall drowse beside thee, so my soul doth ache. "

32

Thus whispering, his warm, unnerved arm
Sank in her pillow.   Shaded was her dream
By the dusk curtains : — 'twas a midnight charm
Impossible to melt as iced stream :
The lustrous salvers in the moonlight gleam ;
Broad golden fringe upon the carpet lies :
It seem'd he never, never could redeem
From such a stedfast spell his lady's eyes ;
So mus'd awhile, entoil'd in woofed phantasies.

33

Awakening up, he took her hollow lute, —
Tumultuous, — and, in chords that tenderest be,
He play'd an ancient ditty, long since mute,
In Provence call'd, " La belle dame sans mercy :"
Close to her ear touching the melody ; —

它們堆列著，閃著豪華的光芒，
清香四溢，沒入幽靜的夜寒。
「啊，現在，我的愛，我美麗的天使，
醒來吧！」波菲羅在床邊低語：
「你是我的天堂，我是你的隱士：
睜開眼睛啊，別把今宵虛擲，
不然，我就心痛得在你身邊長逝。」

32

喃喃著，他以溫暖無力的肘
支在她柔軟的枕上。　層層黑帷
遮起她的夢：是午夜的魔咒
像冰川一樣裹住梅德琳沉睡。
晶瑩的盤子放射月光的明輝，
寬闊的金線閃在毛氈邊沿：
啊，彷彿那封住她雙眼的夢魅
他將永遠、永遠無法給驅散；
他沉思片刻，也墮入悠悠的夢幻。

33

他醒來，把她的琵琶拿到手，
彈出了一支久已沉寂的哀曲，
悠揚的 —— 曲調是那麼輕柔，
在普羅旺斯，*人稱「無情的妖女」：
這樂聲在她耳鬢不斷迴旋，

Wherewith disturb'd, she utter'd a soft moan :

He ceased — she panted quick — and suddenly

Her blue affrayed eyes wide open shone :

Upon his knees he sank, pale as smooth-sculptured stone.

34

Her eyes were open, but she still beheld,

Now wide awake, the vision of her sleep :

There was a painful change, that nigh expell'd

The blisses of her dream so pure and deep

At which fair Madeline began to weep,

And moan forth witless words with many a sigh ;

While still her gaze on Porphyro would keep ;

Who knelt, with joined hands and piteous eye,

Fearing to move or speak, she look'd so dreamingly.

35

"Ah, Porphyro !" said she, " but even now

Thy voice was at sweet tremble in mine ear,

Made tuneable with every sweetest vow ;

And those sad eyes were spiritual and clear :

How chang'd thou art ! how pallid, chill, and drear !

Give me that voice again, my Porphyro,

她動了動，發出輕微的呻吟：
他停住手，看她喘息 ── 而突然
她受驚的藍眼睛大大睜開：
啊，他跪下了，像石像一樣的蒼白。

34

眼睜開了，可是她明明看見
夢中的景象，並未因醒而飛去，
只有一點不同了，這使她心酸，
因為她那夢中純淨的歡愉
似乎已經不在了！ ── 她不由得
淚珠盈眶，不斷呻吟和嘆息；
她把兩眼仍舊注視著波菲羅，
而他呢，兩手緊握，滿目憐惜，
卻不敢驚動她，也不敢言語。

35

「波菲羅啊！」她說，「怎麼，我聽到
你的聲音剛才還那麼甜蜜，
你的誓言還在我耳邊繚繞，
那多情的目光多麼神采奕奕：
呀，你怎麼變了！這麼蒼白、冰冷！
我的波菲羅啊，請再還給我

---

* 普羅旺斯（Provence），法國南部的一省。

Those looks immortal, those complainings dear !

O leave me not in this eternal woe,

For if thou diest, my Love, I know not where to go. "

36

Beyond a mortal man impassion'd far

At these voluptuous accents, he arose,

Ethereal, flush'd, and like a throbbing star

Seen mid the sapphire heaven's deep repose ;

Into her dream he melted, as the rose

Blendeth its odour with the violet, —

Solution sweet : meantime the frost-wind blows

Like Love's alarum pattering the sharp sleet

Against the window-panes ; St. Agnes' moon hath set.

37

'Tis dark : quick pattereth the flaw-blown sleet :

"This is no dream, my bride, my Madeline ! "

'Tis dark : the iced gusts still rave and beat :

"No dream, alas ! alas ! and woe is mine !

Porphyro will leave me here to fade and pine. —

Cruel ! what traitor could thee hither bring ?

I curse not, for my heart is lost in thine,

Though thou forsakest a deceived thing ; —

A dove forlorn and lost with sick unpruned wing. "

你那不朽的眼神，喁喁的話聲！
愛，別離開我，使我一生難過，
要是你死了，我豈不永遠漂泊？」

36

聽了這情意綿綿的話，他立刻
站起身，已經不似一個凡人，
而像是由雲霧飄起，遠遠沉沒
在那紫紅的天際的一顆星。
他已融進了她的夢，好似玫瑰
把它的香味與紫羅蘭交融；──
但這時，西北風在猛烈地吹，
刺骨的冰雪敲打窗戶，給戀人
提出警告：節夕的月亮已經下沉。

37

天昏地暗，冰雪敲打得急驟：
「這不是夢呀，我的愛，我的新娘！」
天昏地暗，寒風在橫掃和嘶吼：
「這不是夢呀，唉！唉！我真悲傷！
波菲羅竟讓我在這兒一個人。──
多狠心！是誰引你來到這裏的？
但我也不怨尤，因為這顆心
已溶進你的了，即使被你遺棄，
像失散的鴿子，撲著病弱的羽翼。」

38

"My Madeline ! sweet dreamer ! lovely bride !

Say, may I be for aye thy vassal blest ?

Thy beauty's shield, heart-shap'd and vermeil dyed ?

Ah, silver shrine, here will I take my rest

After so many hours of toil and quest,

A famish'd pilgrim, — saved by miracle.

Though I have found, I will not rob thy nest

Saving of thy sweet self ; if thou think'st well

To trust, fair Madeline, to no rude infidel.

39

"Hark ! 'tis an elfin-storm from faery land,

Of haggard seeming, but a boon indeed :

Arise — arise ! the morning is at hand ; —

The bloated wassaillers will never heed : —

Let us away, my love, with happy speed ;

There are no ears to hear, or eyes to see, —

Drown'd all in Rhenish and the sleepy mead :

Awake ! arise ! my love, and fearless be,

For o'er the southern moors I have a home for thee. "

40

She hurried at his words, beset with fears,

38

「哦，我的梅德琳！你多會做夢！
你說，我能否永遠受你的福祉？
能否作你的盾牌，牌心塗上硃紅？
銀色的廟堂啊，我願安息在此，
我，長期朝拜的香客，飢餓、疲勞，
終於碰見奇蹟了。但請放心，
梅德琳啊，我雖找到你的香巢，
我不偷別的，只要你的金身，
要是你允許我對你全心篤信。

39

「聽啊！這是仙靈送來的風暴，
它雖然悽厲，卻似對我們祝福：
起身吧，起身吧！一會就破曉；
那些酗酒的人絕不會攔阻 ——
讓我們快走吧，親愛的姑娘，
這時絕沒人看見，沒人聽到，
他們都被蜜酒送進了睡鄉，
起身吧！起身吧！愛，不要膽小；
爲了你，我在南方早把家園置好。」

40

她匆匆跟隨他，萬分地害怕，

For there were sleeping dragons all around,

At glaring watch, perhaps, with ready spears —

Down the wide stairs a darkling way they found. —

In all the house was heard no human sound.

A chain- droop'd lamp was flickering by each door ;

The arras, rich with horseman, hawk, and hound,

Flutter'd in the besieging wind's uproar ;

And the long carpets rose along the gusty floor.

41

They glide, like phantoms, into the wide hall ;

Like phantoms, to the iron porch, they glide ;

Where lay the Porter, in uneasy sprawl,

With a huge empty flaggon by his side :

The wakeful bloodhound rose, and shook his hide,

But his sagacious eye an inmate owns :

By one, and one, the bolts full easy slide : —

The chains lie silent on the footworn stones ; —

The key turns, and the door upon its hinges groans.

42

And they are gone : ay, ages long ago

These lovers fled away into the storm.

That night the Baron dreamt of many a woe,

因為強暴的人就在四周歇息，
也許正持矛在幽暗裏巡察 ——
他們從漆黑的樓梯摸索下去。
整個府邸裏寂然不聞人聲。
每個門前，垂掛的燈在閃爍；
壁上的畫帷在狂吼的風中，
人、馬、鷹、犬都隨著風抖索；
在風過處，地氈一角也時起、時落。

41

他們像是幽靈，潛行到廳堂內；
像是幽靈，他們來到了鐵門前；
守門人正踡伏在那裏酣睡，
一只空肚的酒瓶在他身邊；
驚醒的狗站直，搖搖全身的毛，
但立刻認出了是主人走近；
門閂輕易地一一滑出門道，
鐵索堆在石板上，守著寂靜；
鑰匙轉動了，大門吱紐了一聲。

42

於是他們逃了：啊，在那遠古
這一對情人逃奔到風雪中。
那一夜，男爵夢見不幸的事故，

And all his warrior-guests, with shade and form
Of witch, and demon, and large coffin-worm,
Were long be-nightmar'd.   Angela the old
Died palsy-twitch'd, with meagre face deform ;
The Beadsman, after thousand aves told,
For aye unsought for slept among his ashes cold.

他的勇武的賓客也都被惡夢
久久地糾纏，看見妖魔、鬼怪
和墓穴中蠕動的長條蛆蟲。
老安吉拉癱瘓死去，早已不在；
那誦經老僧，誦過了千遍經文，
也寂然坐化在他冰冷的火灰中。

1819年1－2月

查良錚小傳

　　查良錚，筆名穆旦，1918年4月5日出生於天津。祖先爲浙江省海寧縣名門望族。幼年家道中落，生活困苦，幸有慈母諄諄教誨，自強不息。

　　小學畢業後，1929年入天津南開學校。高中期間，開始詩文創作，顯露詩才，1934年開始用「穆旦」署名發表詩作。年輕的詩人憂國憂民，「灑著一腔熱血」大聲疾呼抗日救亡。

　　高中畢業後，1935年入清華大學外國語文系，開始寫雪萊式的浪漫派的詩。抗日戰爭開始後，清華輾轉遷往昆明，1938年與北大、南開合併組成西南聯合大學，良錚在外文系繼續學習。1940年畢業、留校任助教。

　　在西南聯大期間，受到英國敎授燕卜蓀的影響，開始系統接觸英美現代派詩歌和文論，逐漸形成了自己獨樹一幟的全面現代化的詩風，並成爲四十年代中國現代派詩人「九葉派」的先驅。

　　1941年，詩人以六十行長詩〈讚美〉歌唱民族深重的苦難和血泊中的再生，氣勢磅礴，不愧爲那個大時代愛國主義詩篇中的絕唱。1942年寫的〈詩八章〉則是中國詩史上前無古人的情詩。

　　1942年春，西南邊陲告急，二十四歲的愛國詩人走出學府，隨中國遠征軍出征緬甸抗日戰場。旣親歷了與日軍的殊死戰鬥，又在大撤退中越過重巒疊嶂的野人山、瘴癘橫行的原始森林。官兵死傷枕藉，良錚幸得生還。三年後，這段刻骨銘心的經歷升華爲〈森林之魅——祭胡康河上的白骨〉詩篇。這首椎心泣血的長詩，不僅是對遺屍山野的戰友深情的祭奠，也是紀念千千萬萬爲抗日而陣亡的

將士的史詩。

1945年10月，北上瀋陽，創辦《新報》，任總編輯。《新報》以敢言、敢揭露黑暗著稱，1947年8月遭查封。

穆旦四十年代先後出版過三個詩集：《探險隊》，1945、《穆旦詩集》，1947、《旗》，1948。

1947年10月，考取自費赴美留學。1949年8月抵美，9月進入芝加哥大學研究生院，攻讀英美文學碩士學位，同時選修俄羅斯文學課程。12月結婚，夫人周與良當時在芝大攻讀生物學博士學位。1950年底良錚獲得文學碩士學位。1952年夏，周與良獲得博士學位。

1953年2月，良錚滿懷報效祖國的激情，偕夫人回到北京。同年5月，二人同時應聘到天津南開大學任教。他「衷心希望為祖國的文化繁榮多做貢獻」，利用業餘時間和全部假期翻譯俄、英文學經典。在1953年底至1958年底的五年中，出版了直接從俄文翻譯的季摩菲耶夫著《文學原理》四卷、普希金的代表作《歐根·奧涅金》等多部長篇敘事詩、普希金抒情詩五百首、《別林斯基論文學》等，還出版了英國詩人拜倫、布萊克、濟慈、雪萊等人的抒情詩選。

1957年春「大鳴大放」期間，良錚未發一言，幸免於「右派」之難。但良錚秉性耿直，遇事往往仗義直言，不見容於當局，當年愛國從軍卻被羅織成「歷史反革命」的罪證。1958年12月，萬里來歸的愛國詩人和文學翻譯家被逐出講堂，到圖書館「監督勞動」，從此開始了近二十年的賤民生涯。雖然身處逆境，1962年開始，長夜孤燈，潛心譯述拜倫的巨著《唐璜》，1965年譯完。文革期間，紅衛兵來抄家，大量書刊和文稿付之一炬，唯《唐璜》譯稿幸免於難。

1976年，「四人幫」覆沒以後，詩人十分振奮，詩情洋溢，重

新寫下了將近三十首抒情詩。同年12月寫的絕筆〈冬〉，四章六十四行，唱出了「人生本來是一個嚴酷的冬天」，淒婉欲絕，彷彿是半生坎坷的天才詩人為自己譜寫的輓歌。

1977年2月24日，因腿傷重新入院手術，不料25日突發心臟病，26日凌晨棄世，享年僅五十八歲。死者當年在「監督勞動」之餘嘔心瀝血翻譯的《唐璜》，幾經周折，直到1980年7月才由人民文學出版社出版，立即成為公認的文學翻譯的經典。1985年5月28日，詩人穆旦的骨灰安葬於北京香山腳下的萬安公墓，陪葬的正是一部《唐璜》。

逝世二十週年前夕，《穆旦詩全集》在北京出版。

關於洪範版《濟慈詩選》

　　洪範版《濟慈詩選》是詩人穆旦一九五○年代的中譯，原非中、英對照本。此次以對照方式重刊，英文悉以穆旦根據的 Ernest de Sélincourt(1870－1943) 編校本發排。Sélincourt 在一九二八至三三年任牛津大學英詩講座教授，至今仍以浪漫時期英詩版本學見知於世。一九○五年刊行的濟慈詩校註本雖比牛津大學出版社的版本早幾年，但牛津版未能後出轉精，雖很風行，今天已無參考價值，倒是 Sélincourt 版仍受行家推崇。穆旦選用這個版本，可見懂行。

　　穆旦的中譯原無對照之圖，且譯詩多少牽涉創作，有兩首詩的題目調整較大，分別是：〈啊，在夏日的黃昏〉（第二十四首）、〈假如英詩〉（第四十四首）。此外，〈有多少詩人〉、〈哦，孤獨〉、〈陣陣寒風〉、〈女人！當我看到你〉、〈我求你的仁慈〉、〈狄萬的姑娘〉六首，均略有刪剪，非原題全譯。另有〈燦爛的星〉一首則以英文首行意象為題。至於名作〈無情的妖女〉，以段次及內容來看，穆旦應是以 Sélincourt 本此詩第一個版本為依歸。洪範版的英文即原來的 "first version"。

　　註釋方面，凡穆旦自註，均有說明。原序言明顯受蘇聯英詩研究影響的政治觀點，早已不合時宜，一律刪除。

　　洪範版對照本得以面世，多承吳國坤準博士自哈佛大學圖書館影寄英文原文，現任教香港中文大學英文系的黃麗明博士幫忙校對，穆旦友人巫寧坤教授自美賜寄小傳。

鄭樹森 2002年